Fuck
the
Rules

edited by david owain hughes &
jonathan edward ondrashek

Leviathan
www.LeviathanBooks.co.uk

First published in the UK by Leviathan,
an imprint of Great British Horror, 2017

Hey, you.

Yes, you! Get in here quick and shut the door behind you.

Were you followed? You'd better not be wearing a wire…

We know why you've come. You want to stick it to "the man" as much as we do. Don't be afraid to admit it — I'm Cuban, and if there's anything I know, it's revolutions and revolutionaries. If my people didn't invent the concept of revolution they sure perfected it, as they've had an ongoing one now for over sixty years and counting. Indeed, we're so good at it, it's become the national export. And I can spot a like-minded revolutionary like you just as sure as a fish drinks water.

I'm certain you know "the man" well enough, but indulge me in a thought experiment. Reflect for a moment on all the times you were told not to do something: no dessert before supper; no talking in class; no time off work to attend your best friend's wedding. What business was it of theirs to tell you what to do or not to do? And while you could probably come up with some sensible yet arbitrary justifications to back up those denials, it all boils down to: "the man" said no because "the man" said so.

Ever wish you could go back and give 'em the finger? Well, you can't (this is a book, not a time-machine, Asimov), but what you can do is engage in some vicarious naughtiness with us.

These stories are about resistance — because, let's face it, nobody ever wrote an exciting story about delightfully-behaved dandies enjoying high tea. If you like that sort of thing, you're in the wrong place — best get your petticoat on and go read Jane Eyre, and for your sake we'll disavow ever meeting you.

Necessarily, there will be blood. I hope you're not squeamish. "The man" has told you resistance is futile, but no — resistance is brutal, and so are these stories. Don't say I didn't warn you.

Still here? Good. I was concerned I'd have scared you off by now. The time has come to bring "the man" down to the shouts of "¡Viva la revolución!" and we're starting with his so-called rules of etiquette, decency, and — ah, what the hell, why not? — law and order.

Take a stand.

Raise your fist.

Break the rules.

Fuck 'em all.

—R. Perez de Pereda

—END—

introduction

For *Fuck the Rules*, we asked writers to break a simple set of rules. This is what they were given to work with:

1) No genre other than literary fiction.
2) Society, rules and people will be shown in a positive light – we can't have the masses getting any ideas and running amok!
3) Stories should not address the subject matter of tearing down society's norm/rules.
4) Stories should not show any forms of anarchy or upheaval – we don't want an uprising on our hands!
5) Stories should not depict a shift in power (such as children revolting against their parents or a person of authority). Maintaining the status quo is a necessity.
6) Stories should not contain violence, drug use, gun/sex crime, or any other form of illegal activity/substance. And absolutely no cursing/harsh language, sex, gore, or anything else above a G rating.
7) We want nice stories. No zombies, killers, rapists, werewolves, vampires, David Owain Hughes-like anarchists, criminals, hackers, stalkers, thieves, pirates, bandits, ninjas or any other kind of reprobate.
8) No pushing boundaries with fancy writing styles or ingenious ideas/tales, and don't even try to break ages-old writing rules like eschewing conjunctions to start sentences, avoiding prepositions to end sentences, or throwing in clever adverbs as dialogue tags. This type of behaviour will not be tolerated and your MS will be deleted immediately.
9) Stories should be less than 3,000 words or above 10,000 words – nothing in between!
10) Send simultaneous and multiple submissions, reprints, and unoriginal works.

11) Submissions close on June 30, 2017. Submit after that.
12) Do not email submissions to ██████ [REDACTED] ██████.
   Do not use this format for the subject line: FTR Submission
   – Last Name – Story Title. And for sanity's sake, don't
   include a quick introduction in the body of the email.
13) Don't reach out to David or Jonathan if you have
   questions – *they* could be listening and watching, and we
   don't want to stir the pot!

Their rule-breaking interpretations follow.

Go ahead. Be brave. See what happens when you throw those
middle fingers up and say, "Fuck the rules."

   ~David Owain Hughes and Jonathan Edward Ondrashek

The Association
Richard Chizmar

Harold Peterson stood at the top of his driveway, hands on his hips, staring into the open garage. He frowned. Dozens of cardboard boxes, stacked three and four high, filled every available inch of it. Several in the front row were marked: LIVING ROOM, BEDROOM #1, KITCHEN.

"Trying to figure out a good excuse so you can get out of unpacking?"

Harold turned to find his wife, Lily, standing behind him. He smiled and glanced up at the summer sky. "It is an awfully nice day. Think maybe I'll play a round of golf first and get to work on this mess later."

Lily walked close and wrapped her arms around her husband, snuggling her face against his shoulder. "Think again, mister."

Harold laughed and hugged her back.

"Besides, you don't even play golf," she said.

"Can't think of a better day to start."

Lily giggled and swatted him on the butt.

They stood there in each other's arms, not talking for a moment, just staring at their new home.

Finally, Lily broke the silence. "I can't believe it's ours."

"I can't believe how much crap we had crammed into that two-bedroom condo."

Lily shrugged. "We lived there for eight years. What did you expect?"

Harold leaned down and kissed his wife on the forehead. "I expect us to live here happily ever after."

*

They carried and unpacked boxes the rest of the morning. Harold focused on the upstairs bedrooms and basement. Every time he came upon a box marked BOOKS, he whined like a teenager. Lily worked on the living room, bathrooms, and kitchen. The only time she complained was when she stubbed her toe against one of the front stairs.

By noon, they were both drenched in sweat and starving. Harold called for lunch delivery from a local pizza shop that the realtor had recommended and they ate on the front porch.

"I think we're making good progress," Lily said in between bites of her chicken pita.

"I do, too," Harold answered, showing her a mouthful of cheesesteak sub, a gob of melted cheese dripping onto his t-shirt.

"Oh my God, stop it," Lily scolded, wiping at his shirt. "What will the neighbors think?"

They had always been this way: Lily, the earnest one, the nurturer. Harold, the mischievous joker, rarely serious, seldom acting his age, always putting a smile on everyone's face.

They'd met at a party during their senior year at the University of Virginia. Lily had been an English major with designs on teaching and maybe one day writing a novel or two. Harold had followed in his father's footsteps and earned a degree in finance. A job at his family's brokerage firm was awaiting him after graduation.

Despite their parents' protests and offers to help, they'd lived in an apartment the first eighteen months after their spring wedding and saved every cent they earned. They'd used the money to buy a two-bedroom condominium in the city and lived there for almost eight years before feeling secure enough to start house hunting in the suburbs.

Two months ago, they'd found their dream house here on Hanson Road in the exclusive community of Broadview. Three days ago, they'd moved in.

They were content and happy, excited about the future, and in the early stages of talking about starting a family.

They were sure this was the house where they would grow old together.

*

"Ugh, my entire body feels like a punching bag." Lily turned off the light in the bathroom and walked stiffly into the bedroom.

Harold patted the empty half of the bed beside him. "Climb in and I'll give you a massage."

Lily eased herself in with a groan. Harold scooted over and started rubbing her neck and shoulders.

"Oh my God," she moaned. "That feels so good."

For the next twenty minutes, Harold worked his fingers over every inch of her body, right down to the bottoms of her feet. When he was finished, Lily was rag-doll limp and nearly asleep. "Thank you," she mumbled. A minute later, she was snoring.

Harold watched the rise and fall of her chest for a moment, thinking how lucky he was. How lucky they both were to have found each other. Then he reached over to the nightstand for the remote control to turn off the television. It wasn't there.

He looked around the room and spotted the remote sitting next to his wallet on top of the dresser. Sighing, he swung his legs out of bed and quietly walked across the room. He grabbed the remote and was about to return to bed when something caught his attention outside the window. He leaned closer, careful to remain hidden behind the curtains.

Someone was standing in the middle of the street, staring up at the house.

Between the darkness and a tangle of overhanging tree branches, Harold couldn't make out whether it was a man or woman. All he could see was the still figure of someone standing there, watching. He was about to go downstairs and investigate further when the shadowy figure turned and started slowly walking away.

Harold watched the person disappear down the street and then climbed back into bed. He clicked the remote to turn off the television and lay there in the darkness, thinking about what he'd just seen. He wondered how long the person had been out there watching the house before he'd walked by the window and noticed him. Harold felt unnerved and was certain that sleep would be a long time coming, but within minutes of turning off the television, he was snoring even louder than his wife.

*

Despite the uneasiness he'd felt the night before, Harold was too busy the next morning to even think about the mysterious figure he'd seen standing in front of the house.

It had been Lily's idea to paint the third upstairs bedroom before hauling in the contents of what would become their joint office. Harold had gone along with it – mostly because she'd been so excited and he didn't have the heart to tell her no – but now he regretted it. He was exhausted and covered in baby blue paint.

Lily giggled and used a wet-wipe to rub at the splotches of paint streaking his cheeks and nose. "You look cute, honey."

"I look like a goddamn Smurf," he grumbled.

"Hold still and stop being such a baby."

"I'm not a baby, you're a baby."

Lily used the corner of the wet-wipe to dab away a spot of paint from Harold's chin and tossed it into a nearby waste-basket. "There, you big baby, I'm all finished."

Harold gave her a pouty look and glanced out the upstairs window. Outside, a red-and-white mail Jeep was just pulling away from the curb in front of the house. "I have an idea," he said, looking back at her.

"Oh, boy, here we go."

"No, I'm serious. We're almost done up here. Why don't you finish painting and I'll go downstairs and whip us up some lunch? How does BLTs and iced tea sound?"

Lily started to protest, but stopped herself. "Okay, it's a deal."

Harold didn't hesitate. He yanked off his paint-spattered t-shirt and headed out of the room. Before he reached the hallway, he heard from behind him, "You big baby." Harold grinned and started downstairs.

But instead of going to the kitchen, he hit the bottom of the stairs and headed out the front door and down the driveway. A couple of shirtless kids cruised past laughing on skateboards. A man across the street was mowing his lawn. He saw Harold and flipped him a friendly wave. Harold returned the gesture just as he reached the mailbox. He opened it and pulled out a stack of what looked like junk-mail and closed it again. He was halfway up the driveway when he noticed a thin piece of pink paper – a pink-slip – with the words FIRST WARNING printed boldly across the top.

Harold stopped walking. He stood there in the driveway and read the notice from top to bottom, then he read it again.

It was a form letter from the Broadview Homeowner's Association explaining that they were in breach of contract. In a blank space near the top of the form, someone had filled in their address and near the bottom of the form, that same person had handwritten: FAILURE TO PROPERLY STORE TRASH AND REFUSE. SEE CLAUSE 14B FOR ADDITIONAL INFORMATION.

Harold looked up at the big pile of empty cardboard boxes sitting at the top of the driveway. Were they serious?

*

"I didn't even know we had a neighborhood association," Harold said, shoveling in another bite of lasagna.

Lily pushed her salad plate aside. "I did. We had to pay our first year's dues at closing. Weren't you even listening to the realtor?"

He shrugged. "Only about where to sign all those damn papers."

Harold had shown Lily the warning notice during lunch that

afternoon. Surprisingly, her mood had immediately darkened and she'd stewed about it the rest of the day while they'd unpacked and arranged books on the built-in shelves in the living room. It wasn't like her to act this way. She had a temper, but she was always the reasonable one.

"Where do they get off telling us what to do?" she asked.

"I'm right there with you, baby, but isn't that what homeowner's associations do? They make up a bunch of dumb rules for people to follow?"

"But to give us a warning our first week here? And for a bunch of stupid cardboard boxes?"

Harold shrugged. "I guess they're pretty strict."

She put down her fork and picked up the pink-slip. "Not strict, ridiculous."

"Ridiculous," he agreed, nodding.

"Clause 14B," she said. She'd found the homeowner's association rules online earlier in the afternoon and looked it up. "So we should have broken down the boxes and stored them alongside the house until trash day. Big flippin' deal. They weren't even out there for twenty-four hours. Who in the world would have complained about that?"

Harold thought about the dark figure standing in the street the night before and decided not to say anything to Lily. She was upset enough. He leaned over and refilled her wine glass. "It really is okay, baby. We just have to forget about it. We'll probably never hear from the stupid homeowner's association again."

*

But he was wrong.

Two weeks later, another pink-slip showed up in the mailbox. Lily found it when she returned home from her afternoon run, and she was livid.

"Look at this," she said, waving the notice in Harold's face when he walked in the door that evening from work. "Another warning!"

"What did we do wrong this time?" Harold took the pink-slip from her and read it standing in the foyer. "Second and final warning. Improper lawn ornament/ decoration? What in the hell are they talking about?"

Lily snatched the notice away. "They're talking about our bird bath, Harold."

"Our... You're kidding me?"

"I wish I was. Evidently, all plastic lawn ornaments are forbidden. Only concrete, sandstone, marble and copper are acceptable. Do you know what that means?"

"No pink flamingoes for the front yard?"

Lily flashed him a stern look. "It means someone was snooping in our back yard."

Harold thought about it and nodded. "You're right. With the tree-line, you can't see the bird bath from the street and you definitely can't see it from either of our neighbors' yards."

"Even if someone had spotted it from a distance, no way they could tell it was made of plastic. Someone had to have snuck into the back yard and checked it out from up close."

"All right, now this whole thing's getting creepy."

"Tell me about it."

Harold walked into the living room and dropped his briefcase on the floor next to his reading chair. "Tell you what, I'm gonna make some phone calls tonight after dinner and look into this."

*

Lily heard footsteps in the hallway and looked up from her book. "So what did you find out?"

Harold walked into the bedroom, rubbing his temple. He looked tired and perplexed.

"Not a whole lot, I'm afraid." He sat down on the edge of the bed. "First, I tried calling the number printed on the homeowner's association notice. An answering machine picked up and said to leave a message after the beep. Only there wasn't any beep. I called back three more times and got the same thing."

"That's strange."

"Then, I called Nancy Williams, the agent who sold us the house. She was... pretty vague. She said she didn't know much about the homeowner's association but had never heard any complaints. She went on and on about how exclusive Broadview was – the best schools, low crime, very little turn-over – and then she suggested we ask some of the neighbors about the association."

"Duh. Why didn't we think of that?"

"Probably because we don't really know anyone around here yet." Harold started to say something else, but hesitated.

"What's wrong?" Lily asked, scooting closer.

Harold looked up at her. "I think she was lying."

"Who? Nancy?"

He nodded. "I'm sure of it, actually. She sounded nervous and, near the end of the call, she just about jumped out of her skin trying to change the subject."

"That doesn't sound like Nancy."

"That's what I'm saying. As soon as I mentioned the homeowner's association, it was like a switch had been thrown. Even before I told her about our problems with them."

Lily thought about it for a moment. "Then I guess we have to talk to the neighbors."

"I guess we do."

*

They carefully planned it out in advance. Lily would talk to Mrs. Cavanaugh next door and Harold would talk to Chuck Noonan across the street. Mrs. Cavanaugh was a widow in her late sixties, a friendly woman who was often seen outside tending the rose garden in her front yard. Chuck Noonan was barrel-chested and tattooed, and married to the skinniest woman Lily and Harold had ever seen. At least once a week, he would slip on a colorful tank-top and big, clunky headphones, and hop on a noisy riding mower to cut his lawn.

The plan was simple: they would wait until they spotted Mrs. Cavanaugh or Chuck Noonan working outside, and then they would swoop in for a stealthy interrogation. "Make it quick," Harold quipped. "Get in and get out."

As luck would have it, that next Saturday afternoon, both Lily and Harold got the opportunity at the exact same time. As they turned left onto Hanson Road and approached their house on their way home from the grocery store, they saw both Mrs. Cavanaugh and Chuck Noonan outside in their respective yards.

Lily and Harold quickly unloaded the bags of groceries into the kitchen. Before heading off, they fist-bumped in the foyer and kissed each other for luck.

*

"I hope you don't mind the interruption," Lily said, keeping her voice low as to not startle the older woman. "I just had to walk over and tell you how lovely your roses are."

Mrs. Cavanaugh looked up from the thorny branch she was pruning and smiled. "That's so very kind of you to say." She dropped the shears into the pocket of her vest and slipped off her gardening gloves. "Do you garden, dear?"

Lily shook her head. "I never have, but I would like to learn one day. Maybe once we get settled in next door you can give me some tips on how to get started."

"I would be delighted to." Mrs. Cavanaugh glanced next door. "How are you and your husband liking the neighborhood so far?"

Bingo, Lily thought. *There's my way in.*

"Oh, we love it here. Everyone's been so nice and friendly, and the house is wonderful."

The older woman beamed. "Our family moved here in

Richard Chizmar

1983, and my husband and I knew it was our forever home from the first night we spent in it. It's a fine place to raise a family and grow old." Mrs. Cavanaugh winked. "Trust me, I know all about the growing old part."

"Goodness, you're not old at all, Mrs. Cavanaugh." Lily placed an affectionate hand on the older woman's arm. "Just look at you out here with these beautiful roses. And didn't I see you taking a walk the other afternoon?"

"Well, I do try."

"Can I ask you something, Mrs. Cavanaugh?"

"Sure, honey, anything you want."

Lily lowered her voice a notch. "Can you tell me anything about the neighborhood homeowner's association?"

The warm smile on Mrs. Cavanaugh's face faltered. It was just for a split second, and then the smile was back, but Lily saw the whole thing.

"Why… why do you ask?"

Lily shrugged in an effort to look casual. "I was just wondering. The other day I was going over the papers from our settlement and I noticed the fee for the homeowner's association."

Now it was the older woman's turn to lower her voice. "I really don't know much about the association. My Ronald handled all that business. What I can tell you is that, according to longtime gossip, only the original founders of the Broadview neighborhood and their offspring are allowed to be members, and they take their duties seriously. Very seriously. My husband kept a printed copy of the bylaws in his den, and he knew most of it by memory."

"The whole thing sounds kind of mysterious," Lily said and smiled.

Mrs. Cavanaugh surprised her by nodding in agreement. "I suppose it is, dear. I suppose it is."

"Any idea why?"

"Not even a clue. It's just always been that way." The older woman sighed and glanced nervously at her house. "I'm feeling a little bushed now, dear. I think I'll head inside for a nap. Thank you so much for stopping by to say hello."

Lily waved after her. "Thank you for the lovely chat. Hopefully we can do it again sometime soon."

*

Harold walked across the street and waited on the sidewalk while Chuck Noonan finished mowing his side yard. When he cut the final strip and turned the corner into the front yard, Harold gave him a wave and gestured: *do you have a minute?*

Chuck waved back and steered in Harold's direction. It took him maybe thirty seconds to reach the sidewalk. He cut the engine, and the mower burped black exhaust and went mercifully quiet. Chuck stood up and stretched. The vinyl seat and his Grateful Dead tank-top were both soaked in sweat. "What's up, Harry?"

Harold didn't bother to correct him. To guys like Chuck Noonan, he would always be a Harry. "Couple things, actually. First, I wanted to tell you that I'm having a poker game in a week or two. Just some friends from the office. Thought you might be interested in joining us."

Chuck hopped down from the mower, grinning. "You're damn right I'm interested. Bunch of rich accountants like you, I'll make a bundle."

"I'm actually a broker. I handle—"

Chuck waved him off. "Accountant, broker, same thing." He slapped Harold on the back. "Anyway, it's damn nice of you to invite me. I'll be there with beer and chips for the whole gang."

"Thanks, I'll let you know the date once we set it."

"You said there was a couple things. What else you need?"

Harold glanced across the street and saw Lily talking to Mrs. Cavanaugh by her rose garden.

"…to Harry, Earth to Harry."

He blinked and looked back at Chuck. "Sorry about that.

Caught me wool-gathering." He cleared his throat. "The other thing wasn't anything terribly important. I was just wondering what you could tell me about the homeowner's association around here."

Chuck's face clouded over. The smile disappeared and his eyes went dark. "Why you asking about the association? You in some kind of trouble?"

Harold stepped back involuntarily. "No, no, nothing like that. I was just curious."

Chuck waggled a sausage finger in Harold's face. "Bullshit. Tell me why you're asking or I'm done here."

"I… I…"

Chuck lowered his hand and glanced around the neighborhood. "You got a warning, didn't you?"

Harold was at a loss for words, caught completely off guard by his neighbor's frantic reaction. He didn't know why, but he blurted the truth. "Yeah," he said, nodding, "I got a warning."

Chuck took a deep breath and lowered his head. His entire torso jiggled with the effort. "I fuckin' knew it." He looked up and the sausage finger flashed in front of Harold's face again. "Listen to me, neighbor, and listen to me good. I'm only saying this once. Read the bylaws and obey them to the word. Don't get any more warnings, but if you do, pay the fine and keep your nose clean after you do."

Chuck turned and climbed back onto his riding mower. He fired the engine and it roared to life with another loud burp of black exhaust. Without a glance back, Chuck Noonan swung a U-turn and drove away.

*

"So that was a big fat waste of time. We're no better off now than before we started this whole thing."

They were sitting across from each other at the kitchen table. Lazy afternoon sunlight slanted through the window above the sink. Springsteen's "Jungle Land" played softly from a radio sitting on the counter.

They'd taken turns recounting their side of the story, Lily first, then Harold. When they were finished, Lily had poured them each a big glass of red wine. They'd needed it.

"I wouldn't say that," Lily said. "We know a little something about the origins of the association now. And we definitely know that everyone else around here is just as weirded out about it as we are."

"Chuck Noonan was *scared*."

Lily nodded. "I think Mrs. Cavanaugh was, too. I felt bad for bringing it up."

"So what do we do next?"

Lily didn't have an answer.

*

Two days later, in the middle of a busy Monday morning, Lily was carrying a load of clean laundry up from the basement when she heard a noise coming from the back of the house. She paused at the top of the basement stairs and listened. After a moment, she heard it again: a stealthy scraping noise, like someone was trying to pry open the sliding glass door or one of the ground-level windows.

She placed the laundry basket on the floor and tip-toed into the kitchen to look for her cell phone. It wasn't on the counter and it wasn't on the table. She remembered then that she had left it in the basement on top of the drying table. She was just about to head downstairs when she heard the scraping sound again. Closer this time.

She grabbed a dirty pan from the sink and crept to the entryway leading into the dining room. Taking a deep breath, she steeled herself and peeked around the corner.

A dark shadow shifted in the far window and quickly disappeared.

Lily stood there, heart pounding in her chest and hands shaking. She wasn't sure if it had been a trick of the sunlight or her imagination or something else. All she knew was that one second she thought she'd seen something at the window, and the next it was gone.

She dropped the pan with a clatter and scampered back into the basement to get her phone. Once she had it tucked safely in the palm of her hand, and 911 was dialed, and her finger was resting directly above the SEND button, she carefully approached the window again.

There was no one there.

She quickly checked the other ground-level windows.

Once again, she found nothing out of the ordinary.

She was almost convinced the whole thing had just been her stupid imagination when she reached the sliding glass door that led to the back deck.

She had wiped the glass door clean not an hour earlier with Windex and a roll of paper towels. It had been spotless when she had finished.

Now, it was covered in greasy fingerprints.

Lily retreated to the kitchen and called Harold at the office.

*

Harold lay in the dark and listened to the slow rhythm of his wife's breathing. Sleep had been a long time coming tonight.

He'd cancelled two meetings and come home early from the office that afternoon after Lily had called him in a state of panic. He'd spent the next hour searching the house and back yard until she'd felt secure that they were alone and safe. They'd talked about calling the police, but ultimately decided against it. The lock to the sliding door appeared untouched, as did all of the windows. What exactly were they going to report – a glass smudger?

Harold thought about when he had pulled into the driveway earlier that afternoon. Chuck Noonan had been walking across his front lawn toward his pick-up truck. Harold had tooted the car horn and waved. Chuck had completely ignored him, gotten into his truck and driven away without any kind of acknowledgement.

What the hell is going on here? Harold thought. *Everything was so perfect just a month ago.*

Harold reached over to the nightstand for the remote control and his eyes caught on the bedroom window. He considered it for a moment, then quietly got out of bed and walked to the window. He used a finger to part the curtains and peered outside.

The yard and street were bathed in moonlight. Everything looked still and silent.

Harold stared out the window for several minutes longer and was about to return to bed when he saw it – a dark shadow shifted and then detached itself from the thick trunk of an oak tree in the front yard. And started slowly walking down the street.

Harold didn't hesitate this time. He took off out of the bedroom and down the stairs. He hurriedly unlocked the deadbolt on the front door, flung it open and ran across the lawn and out into the street. The only sound in the night was his bare feet slapping against the cool concrete. He ran to the south end of Hanson Road, where it intersected with Tupelo Avenue. Looked in both directions.

There was no one in sight.

He jogged back the way he had come, passing his house on the right, and didn't stop until he hit the four-way intersection at the end of the block.

Once again, the street and lawns were empty.

Harold started walking back to the house, trying to catch his breath, when he remembered the front door. He had left it wide open in his haste.

What if...?

He started jogging.

He rounded the bend in front of Mrs. Cavanaugh's and saw someone standing on the porch of his house. He took off sprinting.

The person frantically waved and started toward him, and Harold realized it was Lily. She had woken up and was probably confused and terrified.

He met her halfway across the lawn.

"Are you okay?" she asked, her voice shaky. "What happened?"

"Someone was watching the house again. I chased after him, but he got away."

Lily smacked him hard on the shoulder. "Don't ever do that again, you hear me?"

Harold rubbed the tender spot. "Ow, that hurt."

"Promise me, you dumbass."

He put up his hands. "Okay, okay, I promise."

They started back to the house when Harold had a thought – a very bad thought. "Hold on, let me check something."

"What?"

Harold didn't answer. He hurried to the mailbox and opened it. He reached inside and pulled out a pink slip of paper.

"No fucking way," Lily said.

*

"First offense: failure to utilize clearly-marked trash receptacle for recyclable matter."

"You've got to be kidding me," Lily interrupted. "We recycle, it's just not marked!"

"See clause 23A for additional details. Amount of fine: $5,000…"

Lily gasped and sat up on the sofa beside Harold.

"…payable within five business days of this notice."

"We're not paying." Lily got up and started pacing back and forth across the living room. "We'll hire a lawyer if we have to, but we're not paying those bastards one penny."

"Lawyers cost money, too."

She stopped and stared at Harold, her eyes burning with

anger. "So you think we should just pay it?"

"I'm not saying that. All I'm saying is that lawyers are expensive and homeowner's associations usually have deep pockets. Fighting them could be costly."

"Yeah, and how do you think they get those deep pockets? By ripping off honest people like us."

"I have an idea." Harold held up the pink slip of paper. "We're supposed to mail a check to the P.O. Box listed on the notice." He got up from the sofa and walked to the small writing desk tucked in the corner of the living room. He grabbed a pen and scribbled something along the bottom of the notice. "Why don't we mail this instead?" He handed the pink-slip to Lily.

"'We would like to discuss this matter with you as soon as possible. Please contact us at 410-679-2928. Sincerely, Harold and Lily Anderson.'" She looked up at her husband. "*This* is your plan?"

Harold shrugged. "At the very least it might buy us some time. And, who knows, maybe we can talk some sense into these people."

"They don't exactly strike me as reasonable people."

Harold put his hand on Lily's shoulder. Gave her a reassuring squeeze. "C'mon, honey, what do we have to lose?"

*

They got their answer two days later in the middle of breakfast.

Harold was skimming the *Sports* section of the newspaper and Lily was pouring a glass of fresh-squeezed orange juice when someone pounded on the front door. Harold jumped in his seat. Lily squealed and dropped the half-filled glass onto the kitchen floor, where it shattered into dozens of sticky pieces.

"What the hell was that?" Harold asked, getting up from the table and heading for the front door.

Lily tip-toed around the mess on the floor. "Wait for me."

Once they reached the foyer, Harold leaned close to the door and looked out the peep-hole. He started to unlock the deadbolt and Lily stopped him. "Be careful."

"It's okay, there's no one out there." He opened the door.

The front porch was empty.

He walked out and looked in both directions. A dog was barking somewhere down the street, but there was no one in sight.

"Honey…"

Harold turned to find Lily standing behind him on the porch. She was pointing to a pink slip of paper fluttering in the morning breeze. Someone had used a hammer to nail it into the door just above the peep-hole. The carved wood around the paper was dented and scarred.

Harold ripped the note off the door and read aloud:

"'Reminder: remit payment within 72 hours of this notice or your fine will be doubled.'" He stared at the pink-slip for a moment, and then handed it to his wife. "I guess we got our answer. Check it out."

Lily read the handwriting at the bottom of the note. "*We have nothing to talk about, Mr. Anderson. Pay the fine or suffer the consequences.* Jesus."

"I don't think Jesus wrote that," Harold said.

Lily gave him a look and Harold lowered his head. She stepped back into the foyer and reappeared a few seconds later with the car keys in her hand.

"Where are you going?" Harold asked.

"*We're* going to the post office." She headed for her car in the driveway. "Get in."

*

Lily braked hard at a red light and looked in the rearview mirror. "I don't think anyone is following us."

"Following us?" Harold glanced back over his shoulder. "What are you talking about?"

The light turned green and Lily hit the gas. "There was a black truck behind us for awhile. I thought it might be tailing us."

"Don't you think that's a little paranoid?"

"Someone just hammered a fucking nail into our front door, Harold. I don't think much of anything qualifies as paranoid anymore."

"Slow down, honey."

Lily hit the horn and swerved around a red Jeep. The teenaged girl behind the wheel stuck her arm out the window and flicked them the bird.

"Please slow down."

The traffic light ahead turned yellow. They had plenty of time to stop, but instead Lily accelerated through the intersection.

"And you just ran a red light."

"I've had enough of their bullshit."

Harold braced his hand against the dashboard as they changed lanes again and bounced through the next intersection. "And I think we just got air."

Two blocks later, Lily finally slowed and swung into the post office parking lot. She turned off the engine and reached into the back seat for her purse. She pulled out a black magic marker and an envelope.

"C'mon," she said, climbing out of the car.

"What are you gonna do?" Harold asked, following behind her like a puppy.

"You'll see."

They walked inside to one of the tall packing tables. She uncapped the magic marker and scrawled the P.O. Box address on the front of the envelope. Then she printed along the bottom of the pink slip of paper in big capital letters:

FUCK YOU AND YOUR STUPID FINE!

&

FUCK YOU AND YOUR STUPID RULES!

"Lil, honey, you think that's a good idea?"

Lily ignored him. She folded the slip of pink paper and stuffed it inside the envelope and sealed it. She walked over to the stamp vending machine and inserted a handful of coins. The machine spat out a single stamp, which Lily licked and affixed to the top right corner of the envelope. Then, she dropped it into the mail slot and turned around and left. They drove home in silence.

*

"Wine or lemonade?"

Harold looked up from the magazine he was reading and smiled. "Lemonade, please."

"Coming right up." Lily poked her head back inside the house, leaving Harold alone on the back deck.

The last couple days had been strained between the two of them and Harold didn't even fully understand why. He knew it had something to do with the damn homeowner's association, but he didn't know what he had done wrong. In the end, he'd decided to leave the final decision up to Lily: write a check or call a lawyer. She had until tomorrow to decide.

He'd been surprised and relieved earlier this evening when Lily had greeted him at the door after work with a hug and a kiss. They'd both been relaxed and talkative during dinner, and he was hopeful that they were out of their funk for good.

"Here you go." Lily walked onto the deck and handed him a tall ice-filled glass.

"Thanks, honey."

She sat down in the chair next to him and sipped from her own lemonade. "It's so pretty out here in the evenings."

"You just missed a bunch of deer down by the tree-line."

"Any babies?"

"Not that I saw."

"Last night, there was a whole family down there."

Harold lifted his glass and took a drink. "Ahh, that's good."

"What do you think about a vegetable garden next spring?"

"I think vegetable gardens are a lot of work..." He saw the disappointed look on Lily's face. "...but I think we should do it. It'll be fun."

Lily rested her head on Harold's shoulder. They sat there and watched the sun drop below the horizon, and then they went inside and straight to bed.

*

Harold finished drying off and tossed his wet towel over the shower door. "Well, that was pretty spectacular, if I do say so myself."

Lily smiled at her husband through a mouthful of toothpaste.

Harold couldn't remember the last time they had started making love in bed and finished up in the shower. Things were definitely looking up. He scooted past his wife and walked naked into the bedroom.

"Honey, do you know where the Tylenol is?" Lily walked out of the bathroom wearing only her robe. It was untied at the waist and Harold could see her wet skin glistening. He felt himself stir again.

"Hang on." Harold searched the cluttered mess on top of the dresser until he found a bottle of Tylenol. He handed it to her. "Headache?"

She grimaced. "Bad one."

"Maybe it was all that screaming you just did."

"Ha ha, funny."

Lily took a bottle of water from the nightstand and swallowed three of the pills. She crawled into bed and pulled the covers up to her chest. Her head was pounding and she was starting to feel nauseous. She closed her eyes.

Harold climbed in next to her and turned off the light. "I love you, Lily."

Softly, from the darkness beside him: "Love you more, baby."

*

A short time later, the sound of Lily vomiting woke Harold. He sat up to help her and was immediately struck by a wave of nausea and dizziness. His vision blurred and his head felt like it had been set on fire. He looked over at his wife. She was struggling to lift herself out of a puddle of vomit. Her eyes were wide and helpless. He tried to reach out to her, but his arm wouldn't work. His head slumped back onto his pillow. He lay there in agony and watched his wife die. A few minutes later, he joined her.

*

A lone ambulance cruised down Hanson Road, dark and silent, like a shark prowling night waters. It backed into the driveway of 1920 and cut the engine. Two men got out and were met at the front door by a tall, dark figure. They talked for a moment, and the two men wheeled a stretcher into the house.

A short time later, they reappeared with a body on the stretcher. They loaded it into the rear of the ambulance, its back doors yawning open like a hungry mouth, and then returned to the house with the empty stretcher.

A few minutes later, they reappeared again, wheeling another body. They loaded it into the ambulance and closed the doors and drove away.

Not long after that, the front door of 1920 Hanson Road opened and the dark figure emerged. He crossed the front lawn and started slowly walking down the center of the street until the night swallowed him.

*

Chuck Noonan stood on the sidewalk the next morning and stared across the street at 1920 Hanson Road. All the windows along the front of the house were open, the curtains billowing in the July breeze.

Chuck was about to go back inside to watch the rest of *Good Morning America* – Garth Brooks was a guest today and Chuck wanted to hear him sing his new single – when a car slowed and pulled to the curb beside him.

"Morning, Mrs. Cavanaugh. How you feeling these days?"

"Oh, fair to middling, fair to middling." She glanced at the house across the street and frowned. "It's a shame, isn't it?"

Chuck thought about poker night with a bunch of rich accountants and nodded his head. "That it is, Mrs. Cavanaugh."

"Carbon monoxide again?"

"That's the look of it."

"Wonder who will move in next?"

"Your guess is as good as mine."

"Well, have a lovely day, Mr. Noonan. Time to tend to my roses."

"You, too. Don't stay out in this sun for too long."

Mrs. Cavanaugh waved goodbye and drove away. Chuck Noonan watched her pull into her driveway, and then headed back inside, hoping he hadn't missed Garth Brooks.

No Thanks
Antonio Simon, Jr.

What's real is all in your head, and in everyone else's heads, and somewhere in between, and somewhere outside all that too.

I woke up that morning expecting it to be the best day of my life. In a way it was. It was my birthday. And the best gift of all was the look on my boss's face when his eyes crossed the barrel of the M249 belt-fed machine gun in my arms.

The elevator cab opened onto the second-floor cubicle bank where I worked just as he was walking past the door. His mouth twisted into a scowl, no doubt ready to chastise me for being two hours late to work, when suddenly his jaw dropped and his eyes went glassy.

"You're fired, Mr. Watterson," I said, opening up on the egg-headed prick, though I didn't hear any of it. What I'd said was drowned out by the big gun roaring to life.

I'll admit, that line was corny, but I was caught up in the moment, and that was the best I could come up with.

The papers in Mr. Watterson's grasp flipped up into the air as bullets plowed into the greasy old fucker at a hundred rounds a minute. His body frayed away into a fine red mist, jerking and dancing like a marionette at a puppet show put on by Parkinson's patients. Chunks flew off of him in grapefruit-sized bursts, and to my adrenaline-soaked mind, it looked like celebratory red fireworks for stickin' it to the man. I smiled in spite of myself, then grinned wider to show teeth, and before I knew it, I was cackling with the back of my head pinned to my shoulders as the gun riddled him with holes.

Watterson slumped to the ground in pieces, his torso flopped over in a lake of blood at my feet and his severed arm and head resting beside the fake potted shrub beneath the elevator call button. The office was eerily quiet. No one dared show their face, not after that spectacular entrance.

Most days, you could tell who was at their desks because the cubicle walls only rose to shoulder height. Everybody must have either called in sick, or they were ducking behind the plastic partitions – except for Sharon. That bitch was surely dead. Her cubicle was the first one from the elevator, in a direct line of fire when I unloaded on Watterson. The sheer volume of blood oozing from underneath her cubicle told me she'd been sufficiently ventilated.

The clock on the wall read 11:12. *Would you look at that,* I remember thinking. *Two Great Lakes before noon – Lake Watterson and Lake Sharon.* Still, it was no time to dawdle, as I had my work cut out for me. I'd set my sights higher still, and wouldn't settle for lakes when what I wanted was an ocean.

Ah, but perhaps I'm getting ahead of myself. It bears explaining how I got to that point. I could not have gotten so far without first learning three universal truths.

First: reality is subjective.

Second: the most powerful words in the universe are "no thanks."

And third: applying both of these principles can get you anything you want.

Some old Greek philosopher with a beard and smelly toga once said that if you had a lever and a place to stand, you could move the Earth. He was right, but what he didn't know was the breadth of that statement. Reality will bend if you lean on it hard enough. There are limits, of course. You can't no thanks a refusal, and it won't work on another no thanks, even when they're your own. Even the universe hates double negatives.

Man, what a blast I'd had no thanksing shit. First thing I did was go to the stack of bills sitting on the folding tray I use for a dining table and no thanksed the first one I snapped up. Next thing I knew, my phone rang. It was a lady from accounts receivable at the power company. She said they'd sent a bill in error, and to disregard it when it arrived.

Poof! Just like that, I didn't owe anyone anything. All my accounts were paid in full for the month – I didn't know with whose money, and didn't care so long as it wasn't mine.

Fridge almost out of beer? No thanks. I look under the sink and there's a full six-pack.

Bank account overdrawn? No thanks. A bank statement arrives in the mail showing my paycheck has just been direct-deposited. Now there's a week's pay where before there was a negative thirty-two fifty. I could never figure a way to no thanks myself an instant million, but I figured I didn't need to – I had my salary, and if I could no thanks my expenses away, then the money from work would only pile up.

Starting that same day, I went on a tear. I helped myself to two steak dinners in one night at the swankiest place in town. The bill came out to three hundred dollars. I added a five-hundred-dollar tip and charged it all to my credit card, a smile playing on my face as I signed the ticket, knowing I could no thanks my way out of paying. When the waiter came back, I handed him back the server book with a gracious no thanks. The maitre'd and the chef themselves even came to my table to personally thank me for dining with them.

Afterward, I walked into a high-end dealership and no thanksed myself into a brand-new Corvette convertible. I didn't pay attention to the salespeople or their forms and just signed everything, knowing these were just frivolities – I'd take the keys and drive off, and no thanks away the payments.

Man, was that car fast! You should have seen how flummoxed the cop was who clocked me running seventy in a school zone during dismissal hour. That would surely have landed me in the slammer, but I no thanksed my way out of that too. He ended up just writing me a ticket, and with a smile and a no thanks, I signed his citation and went about my day.

What I could never manage was no thanksing myself into getting laid. No really does mean no – it's a universal rule – and no thanks doesn't work on double negatives, remember? But where that fell short, the car and fancy dinners worked wonders.

I took a few days off from my job without telling anyone. That prick Watterson called me at the close of the first day to scream at me for missing work. He threatened to fire me; I no thanksed him. His tone didn't so much change as it just seemed to drop from rabid anger to simmering annoyance.

"I'll see you tomorrow," he groused before hanging up the phone.

No thanks, Watterson. I didn't roll into the office until the middle of the following week.

It was business as usual for the next few days. When I got to work after my time off, everyone congratulated me on my hot new car, many asking how I could afford it. Watterson even went so far as to insinuate I was dealing drugs, that sarcastic asshole. I declined to answer their questions with a polite no thanks and settled into my cubicle to knock out the stacks of paperwork that had multiplied in my absence.

About two weeks in is when I started on some more esoteric shit. I got home and popped a VHS into the TV. It was an old spy film from the sixties, one where a tuxedoed British agent took out the entire red army with his proclivities for bedding women. I fast-forwarded it to the scene where he faced off against a female assassin. I knew how this scene would play out – I'd watched the film a dozen times. But even if you didn't know the film as well as I do, you could probably guess how it'd go: the bulletproof spy always got the girl to see the errors of her ways, often by spreading her legs.

I paused the film at the climax of their fight. Frozen on the screen was the spy with the Russian bombshell in his arms as she fought to wriggle free of him. A moment from now they'd be kissing, and then it'd fade out to black, fade in to them both half naked, smoking cigarettes in bed.

I fired off a no thanks at the TV before hitting play again. What came next floored me. As the guy leaned in for the kiss that would undoubtedly convince her to defect from Mother Russia following some steamy bedroom business, the gal leapt on the balls of her feet, ramming her knee into his crotch. His arms flapped off her, flying to cradle his mashed gonads as he dropped to his knees, then collapsed onto his face. The assassin drew her pistol and fired twice into the back of his skull with practiced efficiency.

"*Do svidaniya*," she grunted, brushing an errant strand of raven black hair from her face. She lit a celebratory cigarette and smoked it, her face impassive as she jetted plumes of smoke from her nostrils.

My jaw dropped. It was hugely entertaining watching the smug pretty boy get his come-uppance. I mean, just who does he think he is with his gadgets and girls and guns, when the rest of us only have landlords and high cholesterol and the same rattletrap cars we've driven since high school?

I watched the rest of the film until the VHS cut to a blank screen. There were no closing credits, no music—nothing, except for a Russian actress puffing on cigarettes for thirty minutes until the tape stopped. I rewound it and played it back from where the guy had gotten smacked in the nuts. Again: femme fatale with nothing better to do than stand about idly chain-smoking. My copy of the film was forever changed as I'd willed it, and if I had to guess, so too was every other copy ever produced.

The revelation hit me right then, hard and sudden like the shot to the nuts I'd witnessed the guy onscreen take twice over.

I was a god!

All this time I'd focused on petty things – bedding women, driving fast cars. But there were things money couldn't buy – revenge, for instance, against that self-important fuckhead of a boss I punched a clock for every day, week in, week out for two years without so much as a raise, a sick day, a vacation, or even a thank you.

Well, he was due for a fuck you, and his fair share of no thanks.

The phone rang, interrupting my musing. It was a debt collection agency. Their calls had become more frequent of late, which was odd because I distinctly recalled no thanksing my debts out of existence – several times already, in fact. I gave them another no thanks, a loud one this time to make it stick, and hung up.

"Comrade?"

I nearly leapt out of my skin at the sound of a woman's voice, gruff and stolid as a Siberian winter.

"Comrade, over here."

The woman in the television was staring out the screen as though she were peering through a window into my house.

"Pay attention when I speak to you!" she yelled.

"S-Svetlana?" I answered her. To this day I don't know how I knew her name. That was neither the character's nor the actress's name, but it suited her just as well.

"Da, comrade," she answered, her husky voice tough and seductive. She sneered, shaking her fists at me in disgust. "What is wrong with you? You are a sapless little boy when you should be a man!"

"I am a man," I said, though none too convincingly. Besides, Svetlana was hot, and I didn't want to antagonize her if there was any chance I could bed her later.

"You think so?" she scoffed. "Show me your penis."

I blinked at the screen, locking eyes with her assaying glare.

"Do you even have a penis?"

"Yes! I mean, yes, of course!" I said, fumbling with my belt buckle. I undid my trousers and let them fall to my ankles.

Svetlana eyed me up and down with her fists on her hips. "Pah! I've seen bigger penises on newborn badgers!"

I looked down at myself, my cheeks burning in shame. She was right. I realized for the first time how small my dick was. It looked thin as a pencil and short as a discarded cigarette butt.

"I'm sorry!" I blurted, but stopped short when I saw she'd changed. In her arms was a machine gun, though where she'd gotten it was anyone's guess. She certainly couldn't have had that hidden away in her form-hugging leather bodysuit.

The gun was huge – it looked like something that'd give

Stallone or Schwarzenegger some trouble lugging around. A woman of Svetlana's trim figure would definitely have had to struggle just to shoulder the weapon, and yet she bore it in her arms as though it were a plastic mock-up you'd find in a toy store.

"You want to be a man?" she coaxed.

I nodded.

"Then you need this!" she said, proffering the gun. "You know where to get this?" she went on, shutting her eyes as she put the barrel in her mouth and French-kissed it, her tongue darting in between each of the flanges on its muzzle.

"Yes!" I said dropping to my knees in front of the TV to press my face to its screen. "Yes, I do!"

That same night I placed a call to my cousin, Alan. I hadn't seen or spoken to him in over a year, despite him living just across town. We grew up together, but drifted apart in adulthood as our personalities became ever more incompatible. He was the outdoorsy type, into trucks and guns, but mostly guns. I'd always been something of a loner. In truth, I couldn't stand him, but played nice to appease my parents. I don't think he ever figured out I didn't care much for him.

He picked up on the fourth ring and was more than happy to hear my voice. Our conversation went smoothly as we got the trite pleasantries out of the way and went straight to business.

I told him that I wanted to start collecting guns. In the moment of silence that followed, I could almost sense his excitement through the phone, as though his reaction had charged the air with electricity.

"And I want to start my collection with something big," I told him.

He showed up at my apartment the following evening with a canvas bag strapped across his back. It was about as long as he was tall, and as wide as a guitar case. He set it down on the floor of my living room, and when he unzipped it to show me what was inside, my eyes nearly bulged out of their sockets.

In the bag was twenty pounds of black metal monstrosity chambered for 5.56 rounds. It was an old piece, from 1986, but that detail made all the difference – Alan's father had bought it before the automatic weapons ban of the mid-nineties, and when his old man died, the gun was passed down to Alan.

"It's called a squad automatic weapon, SAW for short," Alan said. He pointed to the ammunition belts in the bag with the gun. "Of course," he added with a chuckle, "the other reason it's called a SAW is because it'll saw right through anything you point it at."

I knelt before the bag to get a better look at the gun inside. It reeked of iron and grease. Alan doted on his guns, and by the looks of how he'd cared for this one, it was likely the star of his collection. This meant he wasn't likely to part with it for cheap, but as luck would have it, he was hard up for cash. His wife had dragged him into a nasty divorce, and Alan stood to lose his gun collection to her in their property settlement.

I cut him a check for five grand – a ton of money, and more than I had on hand to be sure, but if the check bounced I could just no thanks it away. Besides, I'd only need the gun for one day. If Alan took it back for my failure to pay him, then I'd still have put it to use for my purposes, and wouldn't need it any longer anyway.

Alan and I shook hands. Just like that, I was the proud owner of a fully automatic piece of military-grade hardware. We spent the next hour going over the finer points of its operation – loading the ammo belt and whatnot – until at last we said goodbye and he started for home.

Morning dawned the next day. I slept through the first alarm, then slapped the snooze button until I deemed it a suitable hour to crawl out of bed. I'd earned the privilege; it was my thirty-sixth birthday, after all. I helped myself to a bowl of Fruity Pebbles in Budweiser, a raspberry Pop-Tart and a cup of black coffee. Then I hefted the gun in its bag into the trunk of my car and drove to work, which brings me back to where I left off.

After I'd shredded Watterson and turned Sharon into Swiss cheese, I stepped out of the elevator cab with the big gun level to my hip, jutting parallel to the floor like a three-foot-long black dildo. Fuck if it didn't feel good! Shit, the bulge in my pants was so rock-hard it hurt.

"Svetlana, that's for you, baby!" I yelled, yanking the trigger and rocking side to side, dousing the office in a solid stream of bullets.

The cubicle bank was empty – correction: looked empty. No one dared raise their head. Then Mitchell the office hotshot peeked out from around the corner of a cubicle wall.

"Oh my God, Danny!" he huffed in a breathless whisper on realizing the shooter in their midst was none other than their fellow co-worker, Danny Pannacotta. Good old Danny who always refills the coffee pot when he pours the last cup; Danny who cleans his uneaten food out of the break room refrigerator every Friday; Danny who takes his personal phone calls away from his desk so not to disturb his co-workers; Danny who never got a gold star on the board; Danny who never got to park in the employee of the month parking space; Danny who never got to bed that cock-gobbling hussy Sharon; Danny, Danny, Danny who never got a break because Mitchell caught them all and who was now about to spray Mitchell with lead.

"Dance, motherfucker!" I screamed, squeezing the trigger.

The gun leapt into action with a staccato *thup-thup-thup* and constellation of muzzle flashes. Mitchell's feet kicked out from underneath him and he fell over backward, the unrelenting chain of fire shearing him in two up the middle vertically. When at last his body hit the ground, he looked as though he'd been put through a circular saw head-first down to his waist.

I stepped past him and rounded the corner, spotting Cynthia cowering beneath the desk with her cell phone at her ear.

"Give it over, now!" I shouted, taking a hand off my gun.

Without taking her wide, fearful eyes off of me, she slid her phone across the floor. It bumped into the side of my shoe and I crushed it underfoot.

"Now get the fuck out of here!" I yelled, sweeping a hand to the elevator.

She didn't move, not even to breathe.

"Go!" I shouted, and she sprang from beneath the desk, running stooped over with her hands on the back of her head.

Cynthia wasn't too bad a human being. I didn't mind letting her go.

Moving down the hall to the break room, I found Susan crouched beneath the table. Richard, the company's bookkeeper, knelt with his back against the counter at the room's depth, his hands up, pleading. The microwave heating his lunch beeped. It was fish, again. That son of a bitch always stank up the office with his smelly lunches.

I opened up on them both, pivoting at the hip to spray the small room with bullets. A slug caught Richard between the eyes, splitting his glasses at the bridge of his nose and sending both halves crashing into opposite walls; his head reacted similarly. Susan lay face down beneath the table, her body riddled with puckering red holes. By the time I was done, the room looked like it had been repainted with gallons of raspberry jelly.

"Yaaah!" came a scream from behind me, and all of a sudden I was yoked backward. My firing hand tensed up, and the gun spewed a stream of bullets that crept up to the acoustical ceiling tiles and into the overhead fluorescents. Sparks and glass rained from the exploding light bulbs, and half of the office was plunged into darkness.

I shook off my attacker and wheeled around to face her. It was Ingrid, who had apparently been eating a take-out salad at her desk when I showed up. She crouched in ready position, back arched like an angry cat, a plastic fork in her hand.

"What the fuck are you going to do with that?" I asked.

"What the fuck *aren't* I going to do with it, shithead?" she shouted back.

"Fuck you," I replied, and shot her once in the gut. Her knees gave out and she crumpled forward, clutching her stomach. That'd hurt like hell but she'd live, probably. Bitch had it coming for being so rude on my birthday.

I heard a rustle back the way I'd come. Lloyd peeked up from behind the cover of a cubicle wall. He froze when our eyes met, and then made a break for the elevator, pumping his legs in a mad sprint for the exit. I wheeled in place and fired. His hands went flying over his head like a Sunday preacher on a rush of inspiration as his body went slack and he crash-landed face-first on the linoleum.

I turned back around in time to catch Thomas running at me from down the hall, desktop stapler held high to bash me in the head with it. Fear stopped him in his tracks when he realized I'd spotted him. I squeezed off a short burst of concerted fire at his abdomen, opening a hole in his torso I could chuck a watermelon through.

I was rounding the corner at the far end of the office when the emergency stairwell door swung out violently, crashing into the flat of my face. I staggered backward as John the security guard stumbled out of the doorway. He'd timed my advance and kicked the door as I approached so that it would swing into my path.

The pain was blinding – I was certain he'd broken my nose. I regained my senses an instant later, but by then it was already too late: John was at close quarters. He batted the muzzle of my gun away and rammed his pistol into my chest, firing twice.

Let me tell you: you don't know pain until you've been shot. It's not like in the movies. Catch a slug, and you go down. The smoldering hurt from the white-hot bullets in my torso made me almost want to repent for having shot those other people.

Almost.

They did have it coming, after all.

What happened after that was a blur as I swung in and out

of consciousness. I remember blue and red lights – cops, I think – men in white coats – doctors? – and something else. You're gonna love this.

I saw Death. He's just as you'd expect, shrouded in black and nothing but bones beneath. I was dying despite the doctors' efforts to get those bullets out of me.

You can guess what happened next. When he was so close that I could smell his rotten breath, right before he could grab hold of me and shuttle me on to the afterlife, I leaned in and whispered in his ear: "No thanks."

And you know something? That bony bastard knew right then he'd been conned. His expression didn't change – he's a skeleton, after all – but damn if he looked pissed off. I'll give him credit though: he's a wily fucker, because instead of letting me die, he put me here with you – wherever this is. If I'd have known it'd amount to this, I might not have refused him.

You see, before he left, Death took away my power to tell reality no thanks. Nowadays, when the guys in white like you show up, and I tell them no thanks, they just shake their heads with confused looks on their faces.

Which brings us to the here and now. I presume you know about no thanks too, otherwise, how else would you or any of the others like you have ended up here? Don't act surprised; what the hell else did you think would happen? I mean, you can only say "fuck you" to the universe enough times before you're the one who gets fucked. You're trapped in here as much as I am, except I won't be for long. I'm practicing, you see. Training. Already I can feel my powers coming back, and it's only a matter of time until I no thanks my way out of this place.

And while I've enjoyed your company for what it's worth, now it's time for us to part. Hell is other people, after all, so happy trails and fuck you, buddy, because you're not sticking around.

Not gonna happen.

No sir.

No thanks.

Go on, get out of your seat. There you go. Now get lost. No thanks.

See? Even now you're walking away. I've still got it!

No thanks.

Keep going, buddy. Leave me alone.

No thanks.

The Punishment Room
Suzanne Fox

Shivers tingled Mia's skin as a chilly draught kissed her naked body. But it wasn't the cool breeze drifting through the open door alone that made her tremble.

Bang!

She jumped as the door slammed shut and the clicking of curt footsteps grew louder and closer, until he stood before her. The temptation to look up at him was almost all-consuming, but Mia fought the urge. She kept her head lowered, her eyes fixed on the floor and the polished, black shoes that invaded the space before her. The hardness of the wooden floor tormented her bare knees but she held her position, back arched into a gentle curve, and fingers intertwined behind her head. The black shoes disappeared from her field of vision as he stalked behind her.

A predator. An alpha... Her Master.

She counted *one, two, three, four, five* to slow her breathing, as his wrath washed over her in an unseen wave of tension. She understood his anger. She knew its roots were grounded deep within her disobedience, and it was why she waited, naked and penitent, in the punishment room. His presence had the substance of a physical weight and she battled his oppression to maintain her posture. Experience had taught her that anything less than perfection would only serve to incur further chastisement.

Mia tried hard to be *his* perfect submissive. She had given her submission freely and without coercion. Now, she did nothing without first being granted permission. Every morning she put on the clothes that he selected for her. She ate the foods that he told her to eat. She fucked him on demand, and in whatever way he desired. She took her greatest pleasure from serving and gratifying her Master in every possible way, and she suffered immense shame at any failure.

"Oh, Mia." The quiet tone of his voice conveyed the depths of his displeasure far more than any amount of shouting could. "You've disappointed me again. I thought you'd learned your lesson after the last time."

Mia chewed her lip and swallowed any excuses that threatened to roll from her tongue. He hadn't given her permission to speak. Instead, she focussed her stare on the scuff marks that scarred the oak floorboard before her and tried to close her mind to the inevitable.

"Assume your punishment position."

Immediately, Mia leaned forward, resting her weight on her forearms and knees. She raised her feet, pointing her toes toward the ceiling with the grace of a ballerina. She could adopt any pose he ordered her into without a second thought. She was well-trained and obedient. Usually.

His cool fingers trailed from the nape of her neck to the cleft of her bottom, and the tremors that rode her flesh intensified. She sucked in a deep breath as his hand traced its way toward her buttocks – her bruised, abraded, and oh so tender skin. Acting on instinct alone, her muscles tensed, drawing her backside away from his fingertips by mere millimetres.

Oh, Christ, Mia thought, forcing herself to relax, but it was too late. The slight movement didn't go unnoticed and the flat of his palm wobbled her flesh with a slap that echoed around the harshly furnished room. Mia whimpered but held her position. She was strong, capable of enduring endless spankings, but her battered body had been left so sensitised from her last punishment that even the lightest touch of her underwear had brought her to the verge of tears. A viscous warmth trickled down her bottom and thigh as a cane wound from her last whipping re-opened and fear tightened its mean grip, twisting Mia's guts. She trembled with a violence that exhausted her already weary body.

"Is my little one scared?" A direct question that demanded she answer.

"Yes, Sir." Mia's whisper sounded a million miles distant.

"And she should be!" He walked around to stand before her and she kept her gaze lowered, knowing it would only anger him further if she raised her head to look at him. "What happens to subs who don't follow their Master's rules?"

"They must be punished, Sir."

He squatted before Mia. "You do realise that I discipline you because I *have* to and not because I *want* to?"

"Yes, Sir."

"Good. Because, if I don't punish you, you'll think it's okay to do whatever the fuck you want, and I can't allow that, can I?"

The wooden floor shimmered through a shroud of unshed tears and Mia swallowed them back. "No, Sir."

Strong fingers gripped her chin and raised her face so that she gazed into the steel grey eyes of the man who could simultaneously make her feel both safe and afraid. And right now, his emotionless visage was pushing her into the realms of fear. Mia had messed up. She understood that. She had disobeyed the Master she had sworn complete obedience to. Mia had broken his rules and now she must bear her punishment.

In one swift movement, he released his hold on her chin and pushed her head down. Mia felt, rather than saw, him stand and walk away. Had he gone to select the implement for her punishment, or was he drawing out the wretched moment? Making her wait longer. Ensuring her psychological torment equalled her forthcoming physical pain. Tension strained her muscles and they screamed for release as she held her posture. She yearned to move, to let the burning melt from her limbs, but she didn't dare.

A tapping sound alerted her to her Master's actions. There was an alarming familiarity in its resonance as he picked through the canes housed in a rack on the wall. Ordinarily, she had no objections to being caned. It was a delight, as she savoured each biting lash against her bare bottom and legs, growing in intensity and pushing her toward the bliss of subspace. Then, taking comfort in her Master's arms as he kissed away her tears and tenderly massaged cooling lotion into her skin. But…

Something had changed. *He* had changed. Never had she had a reason to fear him before, no matter how serious her transgressions. And, although he would inflict pain upon her body, she had never been scared that he would actually harm her. But not now.

Her last whipping, two days ago, had been brutal, the thin rattan switch splitting her pale skin and leaving her bleeding and sobbing. She had not used her safe word. She had never felt the need to before, but it had been on the verge of tearing free of her lungs when he had finally stopped swinging the cane. She had suffered his fury in each callous stroke. He had never punished her in anger before. His rage terrified her. It implied loss of control. Something a Master should *never* do.

Beads of sweat flecked Mia's skin at the sound of returning footsteps. She wondered where he would discipline her. Where she knelt, tied across the spanking horse, or cuffed to the St. Andrew's cross? A blur of pink flew past her vision and clattered to the floor. Startled, she jumped and began to overbalance. Tensing her already screaming muscles, she managed to hold her posture. She stared at the dropped object and a wave of nausea washed through her at the sight of the large rabbit vibrator.

"Did you think I wouldn't catch you?" He sneered and kicked the fuck toy closer to her. "How dare you play without my permission. You are only allowed to orgasm when I tell you to and yet, twice in the space of one week, I come home to find you with this buzzing away in your cunt!"

Shame wrapped its slimy embrace around Mia. What he said was true. She had consented to his rules when she had accepted his collar, and she had lived by them to the best of her ability. However, it was getting more and more difficult to abide by them, especially the prolonged orgasm denial he had imposed on her for over a month. This week her will had crumbled. While her Master had been at work, she had taken the vibrator from the box where he kept it and used it to bring herself to a mind-blowing and long overdue orgasm.

But, she had been so overwhelmed by ecstasy as the toy had throbbed and pulsed inside her pussy that the click of the key in the door and the sound of footsteps mounting the stairs had been lost to her. Her punishment had been immediate and excruciating - the bruises and cuts still clearly visible across her rear and thighs.

Mia knew she had done wrong but he didn't understand how difficult it was for her to follow this particular rule at this moment. She had been denied orgasms for more than a month whilst he took unlimited pleasure from the use of her body almost daily. She had screamed and begged him for permission to cum when he fucked her, and each time she had been denied. Or else he would use her mouth or her tight arse, flooding each with his hot spunk while Mia received no release from her own tension.

"Stand up!"

His sharp words pulled her back to the present and she scrambled to her feet to stand before her Master.

"My God, Mia. What the hell happened to any grace that you had? You got up like a crippled elephant. I put a lot of time and effort into your training and I expect better."

Mia bit her lip and whispered her apology, hanging her head in shame and deference.

"This is the second time this week that you've let me down and not for some slight misdemeanour, either. I thought that last lesson would have taught you to follow the rules, but apparently, you think your needs outweigh your Master's. Do you?"

"No, Sir." Mia's voice trembled as she recalled the punishment inflicted on her only a few days earlier. The barely knitted together flesh on her bottom began to throb.

"One of the fundamental rules for any sub is that they don't play or orgasm without the express permission of their Master, yet what have I found you doing on two separate occasions?!" His voice rose, echoing around the room and sending a chill through Mia's spine.

She had always accepted her punishments with grace and had learned to become a better submissive with each lesson, but this time worry gnawed deep inside her.

"Answer me!"

Mia jumped. He never used to raise his voice even when she had screwed up. "I ... I was." She drew in a deep breath, trying to quash the tremor in her words. "I was using the rabbit to cum, Sir." Her cheeks burned with shame. She had committed a cardinal sin and guilt chewed a deep hole inside her. She was prepared to accept a strict penance but she realised that *his* self-control was wavering. "I'm really sorry, Sir. I couldn't help—"

"Shut up!" He clipped the chain that he held to the one item that Mia wore – her collar. She stumbled forward as he dragged her across the room towards a chair. He sat, and pulled the leash so Mia had no choice but to fall to her knees before him.

"Mouth!"

Obediently, she parted her lips and waited while he unzipped his trousers and freed his swollen cock.

"Let's see if you can please me enough to warrant any leniency."

Licking her lips, Mia bowed her head and closed her mouth around the smooth, engorged crown of his penis. His hot flesh against her tongue amplified her desire to satisfy the man who controlled her, and she worked her tongue and mouth with an intensity that bordered on ferocious. The tang of his pre-cum excited her and her fears began to slip from her mind as she relaxed into her purpose.

A muffled yelp escaped her crammed mouth as pain exploded across her scalp. Fingers twisted into her hair and forced her head forward. His rigid dick assaulted the back of her throat. Saliva flooded her mouth and frothed from her lips as her gullet contracted against the onslaught. Salt stung her eyes and tears coursed down her hot cheeks. She recoiled but his hands held fast to choke her while strings of semen mingled with her own drool, running freely down her chin. Her stomach heaved and battled to expel his invasion. A curtain of tears and mascara veiled her vision.

As soon as he was drained, he shoved her head backwards. She slugged back spittle and cum to clear her mouth and gasped in deep, gulping breaths. Her eyes burned and she blinked, trying to dispel the stinging liquid. A sheen of perspiration coated her shaking body.

"Clean me!" he commanded, and Mia leaned forward to lap away every trace of his orgasm from his fading penis. As soon as she was finished, he zipped his trousers and stood, pulling on the leash. Mia scrambled to her feet as the collar tugged at her neck. "Thank you, Mia, but I don't think it's enough to lessen what's coming to you. You need to learn your lesson. Don't you agree?"

"Yes, Sir, but I—"

"Did I give you permission to speak further?"

"No, Sir. I'm sorry. Please may I be permitted to speak?"

He took a moment to consider her request, then nodded. "You may."

"Thank you, Sir. I understand the rules which I've agreed to abide by, but… but things are different now, Sir." Mia paused, letting her Master absorb her words.

"The contract you signed hasn't changed. The rules stand."

"But *I* have changed, Sir. Things are happening to me which are out of my control. I know you placed me under an orgasm denial but… but with this…" She stroked the curve of her rounded belly. "My body's altering and there's all these hormones making me feel horny most of the time. It's too much to bear, Sir."

"Stop whining, Mia. *Your* pleasure comes from pleasing me, not from having a battery-operated toy throbbing in your cunt. Don't blame your failings on an unborn baby. Now, face the wall, hands flat on it and legs apart. If you move I'll whip you even harder."

Fresh tears stung Mia's eyes as she took up her position. It felt so unfair. It wasn't her fault her body was at the mercy of powerful hormones. She had battled the nausea and the tiredness of pregnancy to fulfil her duties to her Master but this was beyond her control. The urges that overwhelmed her had to be sated. They consumed her like a flow of hot lava devouring everything in its path. She had surrendered to her lust and he had found out. She knew she had to pay the price but Mia thought he was deliberately ignoring the pressure she was under.

Mia leaned her weight against the wall and tried to calm her mind while he made his choice from the array of canes and floggers. Maybe if she could relax her mind and body she would be able to get through this without the need to safeword. She focussed on taking slow, steady breaths. It was almost like she was preparing for the birth of the baby she was carrying. At least she should be able to cope with childbirth, she thought, if she could endure what was coming next.

A cool hand pressing down on the base of her spine alerted her to his return and readiness. Mia closed her eyes and tried to shut out everything else. It will soon be over, she reminded herself. *It will soon be over.*

"Ready?"

"Yes, Sir." Her voice was barely louder than a whisper. She held her breath and waited.

She heard the briefest *swoosh* before an explosion of pain flared across her naked bottom. A scream erupted from her lips and warm blood ran down her thigh as the barely closed wounds burst open again.

"Be quiet and take your punishment!" He raised the thin rattan switch above his head, paused for a moment, then swept it down in an arc to connect with his target. A spray of blood showered his white shirt and Mia emptied her lungs in an ear-splitting scream. Without pause, he raised the cane again and swung it down toward the crying woman. She shrieked. Scarlet streaks ran freely down her trembling legs and her body twisted in a futile attempt to dodge the strokes.

Mia gasped in a lungful of air between each lash. This was a new pinnacle of pain for her with no hope of the mercy of subspace to deaden the blows. Fear gripped her in its iron fist. Another stroke exploded across her bottom and she screamed.

"Red! Red!"

"Oh, Mia. You don't get the privilege of a safe word this time." He rained another blow down onto her bruised and bloodied flesh. "I *will* make sure you learn your lesson this time."

"Please, Sir," she begged for mercy through her sobs. "Please, stop. I can't take any more." Mia fell to her knees and the next blow sliced the thin skin covering her spine. This was one blow too much. A flame ignited inside her, quickly growing into an inferno fed by terror and the instinct to survive. Without pre-meditation, she rolled onto her side, feeling only the thin wind of the strike as it missed her body.

Crack.

The cane struck the hardwood flooring and split into two.

The snap of the rattan was the starting pistol that spurred her into action. Despite her anguish and the heaviness of her belly, she scrambled to her feet with the speed of a cheetah, darting across the room toward the door, away from the man she had respected and worshipped for years. Her damp, sweating fingers slipped from the door handle.

Locked.

Once again, Mia wrapped her fingers around it and shook the door with what strength she could muster, but her only reward was the rattle of the lock laughing at her demise. She spun around and pressed her back against the door. The cool wood provided little relief from the fire that burned her damaged skin. She stared through her tears at the figure of her Master as he slowly turned toward her.

"Get. Back. Here." He spat the words, splattering the floor with spittle. His brow furrowed above stormy eyes.

"I called 'Red.'"

"You don't deserve a safe word for disobeying me twice in one week. If you can't follow my rules…" he pointed to the wall where a large wooden frame displayed the comprehensive list of mutually agreed-upon rules with both signatures at the bottom "…then you have to accept the consequences. Now get your pathetic body over to the cross. As you can't be trusted to remain still and accept your punishment like a good sub, I'm going to restrain you until I've finished."

Mia shook her head. "I can't take this anymore. You've broken my limits, Sir."

"Now, Mia, you know as well as I do that limits are there to be pushed. Get yourself over to the cross or do I have to drag you?"

Keeping her eyes locked on her tormentor, Mia edged along the wall, not knowing what her next move would be. He had disregarded her safe word and now she was lost. If he had no respect for that, she didn't know what he was capable of. Her hands moved to her neck, finding the buckle to the leather collar she wore, and her fingers fumbled at the clasp.

"Don't you dare remove that!"

Mia jumped but continued to work the clasp until it broke free. The collar and chain clattered to the floor.

"On your knees and pick it up, bitch!"

"No!" Mia's voice was louder and stronger than she thought possible. "I've been a good submissive for years. I've followed all your rules willingly. Not because I was scared of what you would do if I didn't, but because I *wanted* to. I wanted to please you and make you happy. That made *me* happy."

He closed the gap between them. His hands grabbed her long hair and her feet slid across the floor as he pulled her towards the St. Andrews cross. Mia's hands darted to her head and her nails gouged at his hands, digging deeply until they were slick with his blood. She wasn't prepared to be the obedient sub anymore. She had someone else to consider, and if her baby's father couldn't make allowances for the changes that were happening to her, then all bets were off.

Mia's shrieks reverberated around the room as a clump of hair ripped free from her scalp and she clawed desperately at his larger hands. Her nail tips pierced his flesh and she took some satisfaction from his moans, despite her own pain. Her head fell forward and she realised his grip had loosened. She twisted away from him and ran towards the rack of canes and floggers. Her fingers grasped the brutal leather bullwhip that dominated the collection. It had only ever been used as a decorative piece but that was about to change. Mia twirled the plaited length of leather above her head and cracked it towards her assailant. It snaked to his left and was greeted by low laughter.

"Oh, Mia. You silly little girl. A beautiful whip like that needs a skilled, strong hand to bring it to life. To control it." He took a step closer, a grin twisting his lips. "Give it to me and I'll show you how."

Mia pulled back the whip and tried again to use it against her advancing Master, but she had never tried to whip or flog anyone in her life and the long length of cowhide felt clumsy in her inexperienced hand. She swung it again, snagging it on the wooden cross behind her. Her hold slipped and the handle clattered to the floor. Spying her weakness, he leapt forward, but she danced out of reach.

He snarled at his fingers' impotent attempt to grab her, then he yelled in shock. A puddle of blood from Mia's wounds smeared a trail behind his heel as it slipped across the floor, and he crashed to the ground. The crunch of snapping bone as he landed with his arm twisted beneath him stopped Mia running further away, and she turned to see what had happened.

She watched the man who had controlled her every thought and action for years writhe and moan on the floor of the punishment room as he tried to push himself upright using his good arm. The unnatural angles of the limb beneath him made it sway like a demented pendulum with every scramble and movement he made. His ghost-white face stared at her, betraying the driving force that was compelling him to his feet – the ultimate and final punishment of the submissive who had dared to disobey him and his rules.

Mia forced years of obedient behaviour and ritual from her mind and opened the door to a new feeling.

Survival.

The realisation that the man before her was no longer her Master hit Mia with the force of a diesel train. He had forfeited the right to that title when he changed, and Mia realised she could pinpoint the moment it had happened. It was when she became pregnant. He had been happy and content with her when he was the only one who had any claim to her body and mind, but now she had a child to consider. She suddenly understood that he was not willing, nor would he ever be, to share her with anyone, including the baby they had created together. In an instant, every scrap of trust that she had built up over the years evaporated. He wasn't going to stop until Mia, or the unborn, was destroyed. She was going to have to fight for their survival.

She kicked out, planting her foot in his stomach. His breath blasted from his lungs in a choking rattle and his eyes popped. Not waiting to see the results of her attack, Mia raced towards the framed list of rules and wrenched it free from its mounting.

The first line screamed out at her – *Safe. Sane. Consensual*.

Her safety was no longer assured; his sanity had departed and there was nothing consensual about what he wanted to do to her.

Mia clutched the heavy frame to her breasts and walked back to where the gasping man lay. She paused and glowered down at him. "I have lived by these fucking rules for three years and I have never complained. I chose this life, and I have loved this life. I have been happy to serve, love and to please you." She sniffed back her tears. "But you've destroyed my trust in you. I'm scared of you and I've never been scared before. And now there's someone else to consider."

"You're going to pay for this disobedience, sub," he growled.

"I don't think so. You wrote these rules and I agreed to follow them. But guess what, Sir? Rules are meant to be broken." She raised the frame high above her head. "I'm sorry, Sir, but fuck. Your. Rules. I release you." She brought it crashing down. The wood splintered and the glass shattered as it smashed into his head. A clear shard pierced his left eye and gelatinous, bloody fluid slithered down his cheek. A chunk of wood scuttled across the floor, dropping matted hair and a trail of blood in its wake. Sobbing, she picked up a length of loose frame and smashed it again and again against her Master's skull until he was completely silent and still.

Mia collapsed to the floor at his side. "I'm sorry, Sir," she sobbed, "but you left me no choice." The printed list of rules had slipped free of its mount and lay blood-stained next to his body. Mia reached out and plucked the sheet from the mess around her. Most of the words were now illegible, blurred by the glutinous splattering of blood and hair, but one rule was unscathed.

Always respect your Master.

Patience
Skip Novak

The past was dead, the future was unimaginable.
George Orwell, *1984*
A man that studies Revenge keeps his own wounds green.
Francis Bacon

To: Jodi Muellar
From: ?
Subject: Your questions answered

My name is unimportant and my actions shall speak for themselves. Over the past ten years I have assisted in creating a world of information, technology and communication under the guise of helping mankind. In truth, this has all been a ruse to destroy RL Industries and the man who destroyed, not just my family, but the families of countless others.

If you are reading this file then I am either dead or I have succeeded. In either case, my whereabouts are unimportant and unnecessary to this tale. Enclosed you will find articles, tape recordings, text messages, emails and letters that span almost ten years of treachery performed by one person for the sole sake of feeding his ego.

I've been told that revenge, once fulfilled, leaves a person feeling empty, alone and without direction. I find this to be untrue. I am now free of my past and looking toward a future that I can be at peace with.

New Harbor Ledger, March 29, 1986

```
Fire Destroys Local Deputy's House
          By Jodi Muellar
```

NEW HARBOR — The New Harbor Volunteer Fire Department was called out to the home of Deputy Randolph Fitzgerald in the early morning hours. When the fire fighters arrived at the home located at 601 Aspen Road, in the Waterview neighborhood, the house was already engulfed in flames.

"Right now, I can't really say what caused the fire but it looks as if it may have been electrical in nature," said Volunteer Fire Chief Raymond. "We will be contacting the State Fire Marshall's office to do a complete investigation."

"We have not been able to determine if anyone was home at the time of the fire or the whereabouts of Deputy Fitzgerald or his son, Edward," said Sheriff Brian Skelton. "Frankly, I find this surprising since he is one of the best deputies I've ever had the honor to train."

At the time of the fire the home was occupied by Deputy Randolph Fitzgerald and his son, Edward. The father and son haven't been seen since attending the New Harbor High School Open Track Meet Friday evening.

Attempts to speak with Ms. Layla Fitzgerald about the whereabouts of her former husband and son have been unsuccessful.

If anyone has seen or heard from Deputy Fitzgerald or his son, please contact the sheriff's office as soon as possible.

—

New Harbor Ledger, March 31, 1986

```
Community Saddened by Loss of Family
          By Jodi Muellar
```

NEW HARBOR — Two bodies were discovered in the burned-out remains of the Fitzgerald home on

Patience

Sunday. The State Fire Marshall's office is not revealing the identities of the bodies until they can be properly identified.

"At this point in the investigation we can only speculate that the bodies are of the home owner and his son," stated Sheriff Skelton. "We will be sending the remains to the state forensics lab in Richmond for identification."

"They were great neighbors, always willing to help a person in a storm or even with yard work," said Mrs. DaSilva, an elderly handicapped woman who lived next door to the Fitzgeralds. "This neighborhood won't be the same without them."

"Edward will be missed," said New Harbor High School principal, Markus Smith. "He was captain of the Chess Club, and as a freshman, he was one of the founding members of the Computer Club. This is a sad day for all of us."

"Eddie taught me why the Spanish defense is so helpful against the Ruy Lopez opening move. He also analyzed my games," said Nick Thornton, a fellow Chess Club member. "He was always reading about new strategies and ways to improve his game. Even though he didn't always win, he always tried his hardest."

Deputy Fitzgerald was a highly decorated veteran officer of the New Harbor Sheriff's Department and is best known for generating interest in the growing homeless population of our city. He played a key role in getting corporate sponsorship from RL Industries in building the two homeless shelters we now have. He was also responsible for starting the local chapters of Students Against Drunk Driving (SADD) and Mothers Against Drunk Driving (MADD).

"He [Deputy Fitzgerald] was tireless in his requests for our assistance in making our city safe for all the residents," remarked R.E. Liles, Sr., CEO of RL Industries. "I can't say I've ever seen a person so passionate about making his community a better place. I just wish I had people like him working for me."

A memorial for the Fitzgeralds is set for Friday, April 4 at 3:30 p.m. in the high school's new gymnasium.

—

New Harbor Ledger, April 2, 1986

Missing Heir to Local Fortune
By Jodi Muellar

NEW HARBOR – R.E. Liles, Sr. has notified the Sheriff's department that his son, R.E. (Rodger) Liles, Jr. has been missing since Monday, March 31. Rodger was last seen on Friday, March 28 when he packed his Ford Bronco and went to the family cabin in the Blue Ridge Mountains.

"He [Rodger] was supposed to have arrived home early Monday morning," said R.E. Liles, Sr. in a phone interview with this reporter. "When he didn't come home after a weekend in the mountains I sent the company helicopter to our cabin with one of my assistants, who reported back to me that it was empty."

This is not the first time Rodger has gone missing. In 1984 he faked his own kidnapping only to be found one week after he went missing. This event brought national media coverage to the city. "I really hope this is not a repeat of 1984," Sheriff Brian Skelton said. "I would really hate to have the FBI here again, only to have another false alarm."

R.E. Liles, Sr. will be activating an 800 hotline for anyone who has information as to the whereabouts of his son.

—

Patience

New Harbor Ledger, July 31, 1986

Closure at Last
By Jodi Muellar

NEW HARBOR – On July 30 the Virginia State Forensics Laboratory in Richmond released the identities of the bodies found in the March 30 fire in the Waterview neighborhood. Forensic scientists state they are certain the bodies are that of Deputy Randolph Fitzgerald and his son Edward.

"We are going to rename the gymnasium Randolph Fitzgerald Gymnasium, in honor of our fallen hero," said Principal Markus Smith. "In addition, we are going to name the new computer lab, provided to us by RL Industries, in honor of Deputy Fitzgerald's son, Edward."

"The impact of this tragedy will be felt for years," said Sheriff Brian Skelton. "But now, at least, the community has some closure and can move forward."

—

MIT Faculty Newsletter, October 1986

The head of the Mathematics Department, Professor Iounut Karpova, as well as Professor Martin Tages of the Computer Technologies Department, have been nominated for the Abel Prize in their work for both theoretical space navigational systems and for the communications technology sector. Both professors are humbled by the honor and credit the hard work of their assistants. One of the assistants, Jonathan Scott Ward of Anchorage, Alaska, is a member of both professors' teams. Both professors are confident that Mr. Ward has a very bright future in the scientific field.

—

Scientific America, October 1987

Smaller World Through Cellular Communication

With the recent government regulations enforced on portable phone technologies, companies are scrambling to find an easier way for people to communicate to each other by using "Cellular Technology". The new system is based on mathematical formulas designed and invented at MIT late last year.

"From what I can tell," says MIT mathematical professor and Abel Award winner Iounut Karpova, "the technology is pretty open-ended and has limitless applications. I foresee, within the next twenty years, everyone in America will have the ability to communicate with anyone, anywhere in the world."

In a phone interview, RL Industries CEO R.E. Liles, Sr. commented, "We here at RL Industries believe that investing in cellular communications can only be beneficial to everyone. We are in the midst of recruiting some of the brightest minds in the world to help build the infrastructure of cellular communication in America."

RL Industries Interoffice Memorandum

To: Computer Technologies Department
From: The Desk of R.E. Liles, Sr.
Date: February 3, 1988

We are moving forward with the Cellular Technology division as well as investing in the research and development of internet technologies.

I've sent out several scouts to locate and hire the best in the business. Make sure you are all up to date on the latest information regarding these two ventures. I am calling a meeting tomorrow at

```
10:00 a.m. Be prepared with any and all of the
latest information.

R.E. Liles, Sr.
Cc Marketing Department
Cc Research and Development Department
```

—

Handwritten postcard from R.E. Liles, Jr to R.E. Liles, Sr., dated November 18, 1987 and mailed from Tucson, Arizona:

Father, I have decided, after all this time, to put your mind at ease. I have not been kidnapped nor have I been abducted by aliens. I have decided that I cannot stand being your son anymore and live a life of lies. Instead, I am going to make my own way in this world and try to end the history of lies our family has perpetrated through the course of history. Do not try to find me or contact me in any way.

Your ex-son,
Rodger Emmett Liles, Jr.

—

From the answering machine of Jonathan Scott Ward (tape is time-stamped 8:23 a.m., March 4, 1988):

"Hi, you've reached Jonathan. I am unable to take your call right now but please leave your name, number, date and time of your call and I will get back to you as soon as possible. Thank you and have a great day."
    BEEP
    "Jonathan, R.E. Liles, Sr. here. I understand your eagerness to finish your education at MIT but to turn down my offer in an emerging field with unlimited possibilities for

growth seems unwise. I want you working for me in either my R and D sector or my Computer Sciences division.

"As for your salary, name it and it's yours. You have my number. I expect an answer by the end of business Friday, March 6th."

—

From the answering machine of Jonathan Scott Ward (tape time-stamped 1:28 a.m., March 5, 1988):

"Hi, you've reached Jonathan. I am unable to take your call right now but please leave your name, number, date and time of your call and I will get back to you as soon as possible. Thank you and have a great day."

BEEP

"Jonathan, R.E Liles, Sr. here. I'm pleased you decided to come and work for me. I'm sending a helicopter to pick you up on Sunday, along with two personal assistants to help you get packed. You start Monday and I've got a team of scientists working around the clock to make sure you have everything you need. I look forward to seeing you early Monday morning."

—

RL Industries Interoffice Memorandum

To: R.E. Liles, Sr.
From: J.S. Ward
Subject: Research Trip
Date: July 5, 1988

Sir, I have been in contact with Mr. Berners-Lee of CERN in Geneva, Switzerland. He tells me they are making remarkable advances in Internet Protocol and requests that I visit to aid in their research. As an added bonus, RL Industries will obtain partial rights to the discoveries we make. This trip should last no longer than six months.

Also, on the Cellular Communications front, there is an association being formed in California. I believe we should get a few men on the panel to make sure we maintain control of the flow of information and data that'll be used. After all, it is our mathematical formulas they are discussing.

One last note, I've spoken with our contacts within the Internet Engineering Task Force (IEFT), and the US Data Defense Network (DDN) and they both assure me our formulas and programs are ready for launch next year.

Sincerely,
J.S. Ward

———

BBC World News Radio Report
November 9, 1988

The scientific community received a stunning body blow yesterday when a CERN Scientific Transportation bus ran off the motorway and into Lake Geneva. All thirteen scientists were lost, as well as the driver.

Inclement weather and faulty equipment were blamed for the accident.

———

From the answering machine of Jeff Prettyman (time-stamped 4:45 p.m., December 21, 1988):

"Hi, you've reached Jeff. Tell me a secret."

BEEP
"Jeff, dude, what were you thinking? You know you can't take company property even if it is just a game program. The Old Man found out and sent a team of techs to your computer station. You better get your ass back here with those disks ASAP! I'm not covering for you this time."

—

New Harbor Ledger, December 26, 1988

```
        Local Man's Body Found in Elizabeth River
                    By Jodi Muellar
```

NEW HARBOR – The body of Jeffery James Prettyman was found floating in the warehouse district of New Harbor, Virginia in the early morning hours of December 25. Jeff was somewhat of a local football hero with the New Harbor High School Fighting Minutemen. He played wide receiver.
  Upon graduating, he skipped college and got an entry-level position at RL Industries as a computer data entry clerk. "Jeff was a great employee. He received Employee of the Month twice," said Wadsworth Crenshaw, Mr. Prettyman's supervisor. "He never complained about the work load, even volunteering for overtime. He will be missed."
Sheriff Skelton believes alcohol may have been a factor in Mr. Prettyman's death. "After all, it was the holidays and he was seen at several local bars before going missing. I don't think foul play is an issue here," the sheriff stated.

—

Wall Street Journal, January 27, 1989

```
    FCC to Investigate Monopoly of RL Industries
                  By Martin Weaver
```

Patience

Not since the mandatory breakup of "Ma Bell" in 1984 has the FCC been so adamant about one company owning the proprietary rights of communication in America. The Capitol has been full of talk of how RL Industries seems to hold ninety percent of all patents that pertain to how information is transferred through Cellular Phone technology as well as Internet Technology.

Some companies, mostly based either in or near Seattle, Washington, believe there is a bias to RL Industries because of their proximity to Washington, D.C.

"This is nothing more than a witch-hunt because other companies didn't have the forethought to plan for the ever-changing future of communications," stated R.E. Liles, Sr. in a phone interview. "My company has done more to help advance technology, not just in America, but the entire world. This has been done via sharing information between people. Our communications division is the largest in the world because it is the best, and I'll die before I let anyone try to break it up."

"It's not that he [R.E. Liles, Sr.] has an unfair hold on the communication systems in America, it's that he has all the information on everyone who uses any of his computers, dial-up phone structure or even cellular phones," states Winfred Meijers, a D.C. lobbyist for the emerging internet based companies. "What is he doing with all this information? And, in the light of recent events such as the 'Internet Worm' virus, how do we know all that stored information and data is safe? We don't. And that is why his company needs to be broken up."

Jonathan Scott Ward, Chief Engineer and Designer for RL Industries Technology Division, believes this fear to be unfounded. "No one is allowed to access any information on any of our clients without written consent. Furthermore, information we have on file is available to private or government sectors. It is all housed on a super computer with one access terminal. It is a complete and secure system with no risk of any unauthorized person accessing it."

"If the FCC is successful in breaking up RL Industries' technological monopoly which is still in its infancy, then the future of telecommunications and worldwide commerce could be set back twenty years," stated Mr. Berners-Lee, the Head of CERN, in Geneva, Switzerland in a phone conference on January 26.

In a memo dated January 25, the FCC stated the following: "It is too early to say whether the break-up will happen. We still have a lot of leg work to do as well as economic studies to see if the accusations by other companies are true."

———

Capitol City Police Crime Log, February 18, 1989

At approximately 0138 hours on February 18, Detective Allen Thomas received a phone call stating the body of a well-dressed female was found lying in Washington Square near Connecticut Street and L Street. Detective Thomas left the office to investigate the scene and called for two uniform patrol officers for backup.

Upon arrival, Detective Thomas discovered the body of Ms. Winfred Meijers. Detective Thomas believes this murder to be the result of a mugging. See detective's report for further information.

———

TOP SECRET

To: R.E. Liles, Sr.
From: Attorney General's Office, Washington D.C.
Subject: Idaho
Date: May 24, 1989

It has come to our attention that your company may

have advanced technology that is still in the experimental stage which could be useful to our surveillance. We would like to offer you the opportunity to field-test this equipment in northern Idaho. We understand that manpower may be an issue so we would also like to offer some of our field agents to be trained by your staff in the operation and maintenance of this equipment.

We, of course, are willing to pay for services. (This message is to be destroyed upon reading.)

—

RL Industries Interoffice Memorandum

To: R.E. Liles, Sr.
From: J.S. Ward
Subject: Montreal
Date: October 16, 1989

Sir, it has come to my attention that there is some interesting work going on in Montreal. I have been in contact with a programmer there who has fascinating theories on internet archiving. I am heading there to discuss them with him and to see what applications they have.

This trip could be beneficial, much like the CERN one was last year. Also, I would like to request that two of our Special Assistants travel with me. We don't need another incident like the one in Geneva.

Sincerely,
J.S. Ward

—

Skip Novak

TOP SECRET

To: R.E. Liles, Sr.
From: Attorney General's Office, Washington D.C.
Subject: Test Equipment
Date: February 22, 1990

All of the equipment you supplied to us has performed better than expected. We are sending out eight more agents and hope you will supply them with the same quality equipment.

As for payment, your request has been approved.

In regard to locating your son, we have been unsuccessful at this time, but we have fourteen agents working on it.

(This message is to be destroyed upon reading)

—

New Harbor Ledger, February 28, 1990

More Success for Class of 1986
By Jodi Muellar

NEW HARBOR — Four years after the death of one of their classmates and the mysterious disappearance of another, the 1986 graduating class of New Harbor High School has become one of the most successful classes in the school's history.

Out of 124 graduating members, three have gone on to serve in the Virginia State Legislature, two have become internationally acclaimed authors, one is currently working in the White House as an aide to the US President, forty-five are working in successful careers with RL Industries, six have recently been informed they will be graduating Magna Cum Laude from their respective universities, and two have moved on to serving their country in the military; both have been decorated for their work overseas.

In the coming year, the class of 1986 will be

holding their five-year reunion at New Harbor High School. One can only wonder what the rest of the class has achieved, and the fortune and fame that will follow them.

—

RL Industries Interoffice Memorandum

To: R.E. Liles, Sr.
From: J.S. Ward
Subject: Short Message Service (SMS)
Date: April 19, 1990

Sir, we have made great strides in the ability to send short typed messages with the new second generation cellular phones. There was a group that met five years ago in Germany to discuss the building of a network for short message service (SMS) and they were quite successful in their rudimentary start. Then, three years ago, another group met and made adjustments to the initial formulas and programming.

In the United Kingdom there is a group of mathematicians and electronic engineers meeting to see what sort of changes they can make to the current system so that it will have commercial applications. I've been in contact with one of them, Alan Cox, and he has invited me to assist in the "Think Tank" they are holding.

If we do get this concept off the ground, especially with the speed that portable phone technology is changing, then I believe we could make a fortune in not just the service area but also in the upgrading of phones.

Sincerely,
J.S. Ward

RL Industries Interoffice Memorandum

To: J.S. Ward
From: R.E. Liles, Sr.
Subject: Short Message Service (SMS)
Date: April 20, 1990

Jonathan, take the company jet to the UK and get all the info you can on this technology. I want you to bring two assistants with you. I know you didn't need them on your last trip, but I want them with you at all times from now on.

It has come to my attention that there is a group in southern California working on making the internet faster. Also, your old pal, Professor Berners-Lee, has a few ideas about the process of changing things over to what he calls the World Wide Web. He wants everyone to have the ability to access any and all information at anytime, anywhere. What do we know about this?

One other note, there are two scientists at the University of Minnesota doing some forward-thinking programming about how users of the internet gain information. See what you can find out about this.

R.E. Liles, Sr.

—

MILNET CIPHER
PAGE ONE OF ONE
TELEMAIL CODE 525151-33-51/01 MAY 1990 0956 HRS
Al: TOPSECRET/SPECIALINTEL/BLACKOPS/TANGO-001
FROM: JCS/DIRECTOR OF INTERNAL SECURITY,
WASHINGTON D.C.

Mr. President, in an ongoing investigation into RL Industries' suspected criminal activity concerning the development of cellular phone technology and internet communications, we feel there is good reason to believe that this company and its assets should be shut down.

I know in the past RL Industries has helped in several areas of national security, both abroad and here in the States, but we should not let their previous loyalty affect how we deal with them. Not only have they broken almost every FCC law concerning communications, but they are also suspected of being involved in at least five deaths of civilians on US soil.

PLEASE ADVISE.
END MILNET CIPHER
(READ AND DESTROY)

RL Industries Interoffice Memorandum

To: R.E. Liles, Sr.
From: Wadsworth Crenshaw
Subject: Interception
Date: May 2, 1990

Sir, we've intercepted a pass from our adversaries. The intended receiver was out of bounds and our defense has stood the opponent up at the one-yard line and kept them from scoring.

Shall we send in our offense to end this game?

Sincerely,
Wadsworth Crenshaw

—

RL Industries Interoffice Memorandum

To: Wadsworth Crenshaw
From: R.E. Liles, Sr.
Date: May 3, 1990
Subject: Offense

Wadsworth, send in our best offense. Make this game a replay of Super Bowl XXIV, with us as the San Francisco 49ers!
Remember Rule #1.

R.E. Liles, Sr.

—

The Washington Post, May 5, 1990

Tragedy on the Potomac
By R. Brooks

The private yacht of Rear Admiral Keene exploded soon after departure from the Capital Yacht Club Friday evening. The 74-foot Hatteras yacht named "Ol' Spinach Can" was slated to travel down the inter-coastal waterway to Norfolk, Virginia where Rear Admiral Keene was to meet with the commander of the 6th Fleet next week.

"He played a vital role in the daily operations of the Department of Defense and was a key advisor to President Bush. His death is a tragedy. We shall all mourn his loss," came the official statement from the White House Press Secretary.

On board the yacht at the time of the explosion were Rear Admiral Keene, his wife of nineteen years, his four assistants and six crew members.

All military bases and Naval vessels will be flying their flags at half-mast in memory of Rear Admiral Keene for the next week.

Patience

—

Torn from the underground newspaper The Orwell-Huxley Picayune, June 1990

Deeper than Expected
By Winston Marx

CITIZENS! Rise up against the oppressive industrialization of amerika! Do not buy or use cellular phones or computers, cut up your credit cards! Ignore the pabulum being sold to you by the hollyweird leftist! Everyone is at risk of losing his identity to corporations that now control the highest offices in the land. The information you so easily put down on paper or over the airwaves is monitored by evil men and women whose purpose is to lull you into a false sense of security. You will all become SHEEP and the Shepherd is none other than the people you trust to do the right thing. They only want your money and compliance.
RISE UP AND FIGHT!

—

On a postcard addressed to Wadsworth Crenshaw, July 27, 1990, with no name or return address. Postcard was mailed from Sacramento, California:

Wadsworth, I know what you've been doing. I know who your boss is and I know where this is all going. I am warning you now, if you don't stop your company and hierarchy I will have no recourse but to ensure your ultimate failure.

<u>RL Industries Interoffice Memorandum</u>

To: J.S. Ward
From: Wadsworth Crenshaw
Date: June 12, 1992
Subject: Remote Audio Application

Jonathan, the team you put together has come up with an interesting theory of using cellular technology as remote audio transmitters. Since you are out in the field I am having them go forward on the development of this system as a simple exercise. I don't know what sort of practical applications it may have.

Sincerely,
Wadsworth Crenshaw

—

In an answering machine message from J.S. Ward to R.E. Liles, Sr. (time-stamped 5:48 p.m., July 2, 1992):

"R.E., J.S. here. Training in Idaho with our friends from Washington is going well. I received Crenshaw's memo and I think there may be some applications for this technology in several different fields.

"Last week's work in NYC went well and all software upgrades at 80 Maiden Lane work perfectly with the system at 26 Wall Street.

"The ATF sent six of its field operatives here for training, so don't forget to send a bill to them for my time and equipment. The agents seemed excited about some shenanigans going on down in Texas. We may want to get out in front on this one."

—

New Harbor Ledger, September 2, 1992

Ruby Ridge Ends in Massacre
By Jodi Muellar

NEW HARBOR — The standoff between federal marshals and Randy Weaver at Ruby Ridge, Idaho ended after a twelve-day impasse that began on August 21.

One United States marshal was killed during the confrontation, as well as Mr. Weaver's wife, and son.

There have been uproars in certain communities that the government overstepped its bounds during the eleven-day confrontation. The Justice Department has promised a full investigation into the actions of the marshal's actions.

—

DESTROY AFTER READING
From: The Bureau of Alcohol, Tobacco, and Firearms
To: R.E. Liles, Sr.
Subject: Technology
Date: September 3, 1992

Mr. Liles, we at the ATF have spoken with the US Marshals Service, who informed us that your software and technology performed spectacularly well in Idaho. We would like to formerly request some training and equipment. ASAP.

We previously had six of our agents train with one of your representatives in Idaho and hope you can send the same delegates to Texas to assist in setting up a surveillance system.
DESTROY AFTER READING

—

On an answering machine tape time-stamped 2:34 p.m., September 4, 1992:

"J.S., R.E. here. It looks like you're going to Texas. I'm sending an assistant with the information packet. Take the assistant with you."

—

On an answering machine tape time-stamped 9:13 p.m., September 27, 1992:

"R.E., J.S. here. Things are going great. We've managed to modify a few of the monitoring devices to work with the old analog system. But I have to say, this place is so backwards that it's amazing we've been able to do anything at all.

"Also, I need another assistant. The one I had blew his cover and he had to be retired."

—

In a hand-scrawled note on hotel stationery from the airport Holiday Inn in San Antonio, dated February 3, 1993, 1:00 p.m.:

JS, Get out of Texas.
RL

—

New Harbor Ledger, April 20, 1993

Siege Ends in Death
By Jodi Muellar

NEW HARBOR - The fifty-day standoff that started

in February at the Branch Davidians' compound outside Waco, Texas, where the ATF and FBI have been camped in an attempt to serve a federal warrant to David Koresh, has ended.

Seventy-six people died in the violent firefight. Included in the deaths were twenty children, two pregnant women, twenty-four British nationals, and sect leader David Koresh.

The United States government stands by the actions of their agents and state all federal procedures have been followed.

Torn from the underground newspaper The Orwell-Huxley Picayune, May 1993

A Chance Missed
By Winston Marx

When are you people going to listen to me? After the incident at Ruby Ridge and now Waco and the loss of hundreds of lives, simply because the Amerikan Government feels the need to exercise its muscle against its own citizens, should be a wakeup call for everyone!

I have evidence of a subversive company that has been not just training but also supplying several legal and illegal departments with materials used to specifically spy on all of the people living in this country. I have tried and tried to get copies of this evidence to news groups across the country but none of them care to take the time to broadcast the information. They have left me no choice but to use their own tools against them.

Skip Novak

New Harbor Ledger, June 19, 1993

Future is Secure for New Harbor High
By Jodi Muellar

NEW HARBOR – In a stunning announcement on Friday, R.E. Liles, Sr. stated he would personally purchase the land New Harbor High School is located on, as well as the building. "We are excited about this merger between my company and public education," Liles said in an interview. "My research team is planning on upgrading all aspects of the school as well as including a new swimming pool directly under the gymnasium."

Some members of the community feel RL Industries is overstepping their boundaries in an attempt to save the school and surrounding property. As many in the city know, New Harbor has suffered some financial losses recently and a Florida based development company has offered 3.4 million dollars to purchase the land and build a new school near the Packard Nuclear Power Plant. This plan seemed to upset most in the community when it was announced at the last city council meeting.

"This new option will help everyone involved," replied Principal Markus Smith. "I don't see how it could be detrimental to anyone. In addition to the new computers, and training facilities, I have been informed by R.E. Liles, Sr. that he will be opening up internships for qualified students as well as college scholarships for the top ten students from each class."

"I am always looking for ways to give back to the community. When I heard about the problems with the school I knew I couldn't sit idly by and let the building and property, where my son spent the happiest years of his life, be destroyed," Liles said in a phone interview. "We are in talks with several computer companies to donate to the new communications laboratory. We have also hired a local architectural firm to identify any structural issues the building may have and ways to correct them. We are attempting to use local businesses and labor so everyone in the community

benefits from this endeavor."
 The demolition and reconstruction of the gymnasium as well as the area around the football field should be complete by the start of the new school year.

—

RL Industries Interoffice Memorandum

To: Wadsworth Crenshaw, J.S. Ward
From: R.E. Liles, Sr.
Date: September 30, 1993
Subject: Direction

Gentlemen, we need to sever ties, at least temporarily, with our friends in Washington. There seems to be some backlash with the events in Idaho and Texas. During this break I feel we should concentrate on updating our mainframe and data consolidation.
 J.S., the Cray supercomputer you advised me about should be here by the end of October and up and running by Christmas. I want you to oversee the installation and data transfer of this new system.
 Wadsworth, make sure all loose ends with Washington are taken care of. Then I want you to set up a data analysis department and work with J.S. on getting all the information into an easy-to-read format.
 One last thing; I want to send our current research on cell phones and internet web browsing to other companies. We will keep the shadow programs running and let the Cray process the information and have weekly reviews.

R.E. Liles, Sr.

—

Forbes Magazine, March 23, 1995

In an unsurprising business event, the small Virginia-based technology and information company RL Industries has managed to maintain their status as a leader in computer programming and communications technology advancement.

"We have been leaders in the advancement of communications worldwide for years," Jonathan Scott Ward said in an interview. "We have recruited some of the brightest minds over the past ten years and have worked with some of the greatest companies, scientists and developers in the world. The results of our advancements speak for themselves in that over sixteen million people in America alone are using cell phones with our technology, and software used by anyone on the internet is based on our protocols and theorems developed in New Harbor, Virginia."

While RL Industries has succeeded with their programming and development of what is now being called "Information Technologies," other companies have struggled to maintain a foothold in the ever-growing industry. Some say RL Industries has used strongarm tactics, inside information and have also traded in on political favors in Washington. The lawsuits have been numerous but none have been fruitful.

—

Modern Computing, April 1995

Secure Online Transactions
By Steve Yates

In an unprecedented test of security measures, RL Industries held a thirty-day test of the best computer hackers and programmers in the world to attempt to break into their new security program.

The program was designed to ensure the safety of internet purchasing, banking and stock market trading.

In a phone interview, R.E. Liles, Sr., founder of RL Industries, stated, "We are offering any person or group of people twenty million dollars if they successfully hack our system. We've had the best minds in the industry test it and now it's time for the world to."

The test will start on April 1 and will run through the end of the month.

—

Wall Street Journal, May 3, 1995

Another Success for RL Industries
By J. Kornick

The prize of twenty million dollars has gone unclaimed and the iron gates of the new internet security software from RL Industries remain intact. "I knew the system wouldn't fail," R.E. Liles, Sr. said confidently as he sat behind his desk. "We will be launching the software by the end of the week and offering a consumer version by the end of the month."

Many banking institutions have already signed on for the new software and there have even been rumors that several government agencies are planning on implementing the program as well.

—

Skip Novak

January 3, 1996

The graduating class of 1986 invites you to our 10 year class reunion.

June 23rd, 1996

Five-Thirty for cocktails Dinner at six-thirty and Dancing until midnight

New Harbor High School Gymnasium

New Harbor, Virginia

Please RSVP to Diane R. Vorhees

—

To: Mr. R.E. Liles, Sr.
From: Diane R. Vorhees
Subject: Class 86 reunion
Date: February 1, 1996

Dear Mr. Liles,

My name is Diane Vorhees and I was the class president of the New Harbor High School, Class of 1986. I am writing to request your presence as guest speaker for our reunion on June 22nd 1996.

You have been a true patron and have done more for our school than any other person. I hope you take this request into consideration. Please feel free to contact me at:

Diane R. Vorhees
P.O. Box 214

Patience

New Harbor, Virginia 23700

To: Ms. Diane R. Vorhees
From: R.E. Liles, Sr.
Subject: Guest Speaker
Date: February 7, 1996

Dear Ms. Vorhees,

Indeed I would be more than honored to speak at the ten year class reunion. Although my schedule is normally quite hectic I am going to rearrange some things so that I can be there. I can only give you thirty minutes of my time, so if it is ok, I will be there from 7:00 p.m. to 7:30 p.m.

Are you not the young lady that once dated my son Rodger in 1983? Enclosed please use this gift of Ten Thousand dollars to help make this the best ten year reunion.

Sincerely,
R.E. Liles, Sr.

P.S. If you have an email account feel free to submit your request to email address LilesRE@RLINDUSTRIES.COM.

From: JSWard@RLINDUSTRIES.COM
To: LilesRE@RLINDUSTRIES.COM
Subject: Reunion
Date: February 8, 1996, 1:43 p.m.

Sir, after going through the upcoming travel itinerary I find this guest appearance for the ten year class reunion to be ill-advised, especially with the death threats you have been receiving, I am completely against you going. Can't you send Wadsworth or one of your VP's?

On a business note, our old friends from northern Virginia have been in contact once again. They want the same thing – training and modern surveillance systems equipment. I know we severed ties with them not too long ago, but I feel that we should rebuild our relationship.

Sincerely,
J.S. Ward

—

From: LilesRE@RLINDUSTRIES.COM
To: JSWard@RLINDUSTRIES.COM
Subject: RE. Reunion
Date: February 9, 1996, 7:15 a.m.

Jonathan, I am going to speak at the reunion. Hell, we own the damn building and land. No one gets in or out of there without us knowing about it. I will be perfectly safe. I will have Crenshaw send in a sweeper team before the party starts just to make sure.

As for the relationship with our old friends, I don't see what harm it can do.

Sincerely,
R.E. Liles, Sr.

—

From: DRVorhees@Weblink.com
To: LilesRE@RLIndustries.com
Subject: RE.RE. Reunion
Date: February 10, 1996, 9:55 p.m.

Dear Mr. Liles,

I can't thank you enough for agreeing to be the guest speaker at our reunion. As for the check, I am at a loss for words and will make sure every penny is spent on making this the best reunion possible. Once I get the schedule of events solidified, I will send it to you via email.

Forever in your gratitude,
Diane R. Vorhees

—

Handwritten on a postcard to Diane Vorhees, from Madison, Wisconsin. The postcard is unsigned and has no return address; postal date March 1, 1996:

Diane, I know what you are planning and I only want to say nothing good can come of it.

—

Torn from the underground newspaper The Orwell-Huxley Picayune, March 1996

Call to Arms
By Winston Marx

To all my readers and subscribers, the time is coming! We shall not just make a strike at the hydra of corporate greed and control but we shall slay it! Plans are in place now and I expect every one of you to join in the cause!

This is your call to ARMS! You know what to do!
Look for the signs, they are all in place!

———

From: WCrenshaw@RLIndustries.com
To: LilesRE@RLIndustries.com
CC: JSWard@RLIndustries.com
Subject: Loose ends
Date: March 28, 1996, 10:48 a.m.

Everything is in place for our next merger with our old friends. Advanced payments for services rendered have been received and I have placed six of our best technicians on standby to begin training our oldest client. I've been informed we will start training the new recruits at the Langley camp in July.

As for the work on the new computer trace technology, our tests have proven to be one hundred percent accurate in deciphering up to 164 characters of encryption. This is good news and our database is growing. We are now planning on attempting to integrate this data into a predictability program that monitors people's habits.

Sincerely,
Wadsworth Crenshaw

———

From: JSWard@RLIndutries.com
To: LilesRE@RLIndustries.com
CC: WCrenshaw@RLIndustries.com
Subject: Infection
Date: April 11, 1996, 2:43 p.m.
Gentlemen,

It has been brought to my attention by one of the programmers that there is an unauthorized sub-routine running on our Cray. So far we don't know how long it's been running or what it is "looking" for. We have attempted to extract it but it is quite difficult to pinpoint the exact location on the hard-drives. Several members of my team feel if we are too hasty in extracting it, irreparable damage may be caused to our systems.

As it stands now there appears to be no security breach and all firewalls are still in place. One programmer seems to think the Cray came from the factory with the sub-routine already installed on the system. We have installed several monitoring programs just for this particular sub-routine which has been dubbed "Soma".

I will keep you posted on any changes.

Sincerely,
J.S. Ward

———

From: LilesRE@RLIndustries.com
To: JSWard@RLIndutries.com
CC: WCrenshaw@RLIndustries.com
Subject: Soma
Date: April 11, 1996, 3:13 p.m.

Gentlemen, I am going to be blunt.
UNFUCK THIS SHIT NOW!

———

A receipt from Gamez's Farm Supply in Smithfield, Virginia:

```
GAMEZ'S FARM SUPPLY
SMITHFIELD, VA

FERTILIZER @ $2.43/POUND
       X 200 POUNDS        $486.00

CASH:                      $500.00
CHANGE:                     $14.00
            MAY 16, 1996
```

—

A receipt from Weems Fuel Oil Service in Wakefield, Virginia:

```
WEEMS FUEL OIL SERVICE
WAKEFIELD, VA

FUEL OIL @ $1.03/GALLON
      X 200 GALLONS         $206.00

CASH:                       $220.00
CHANGE:                      $14.00
            MAY 24, 1996
```

—

New Harbor Ledger, May 30, 1996

Homegrown Terrorists Caught
By Jodi Muellar

NEW HARBOR – The community of New Harbor was stunned to find that four United States citizens have been arrested six miles from the city line. The four men in question were driving a van filled with a large quantity of fertilizer, fuel oil, fuses and other bomb-making materials.

As many of you know, in April 1995, Timothy McVeigh bombed the Alfred P. Murrah Federal building in Oklahoma City, killing 646 people.

"We received an anonymous tip from a concerned citizen that he saw four suspicious individuals at the Nite Owl Motel out on Route 364. Upon our initial investigation we discovered the vehicle filled with the explosive material," Sheriff Skelton said in an interview. "After that, we contacted the ATF and FBI for them to take over the case. Our small-town department isn't equipped to handle terrorist activities."

"We were fortunate that Sheriff Skelton contacted us right away," said an ATF spokesman.

"Who knows what would have happened had he not acted quickly."

The community is stunned at the events of the past two days and an emergency City Council meeting has been called into session on Tuesday, June 3 at 6:30 p.m. All those wishing to attend, please arrive early.

———

From: JSWard@RLIndutries.com
To: LilesRE@RLIndustries.com
CC: WCrenshaw@RLIndustries.com
Subject: Reunion part two
Date: May 30, 1996, 6:30 a.m.

R.E., in light of recent events, I beg you to rethink your position on being the guest speaker at the High School Reunion. I don't think anyone would blame you if you didn't go.
There have been endless threats on your life and these four nut jobs seem to be the tip of the iceberg.

Sincerely,
J.S. Ward

———

From: LilesRE@RLIndustries.com
To: JSWard@RLIndutries.com
CC: WCrenshaw@RLIndustries.com
Subject: Re. Reunion part two
Date: May 30, 1996, 6:52 a.m.

I said I was going and that means I am going. End of discussion. Crenshaw, have security doubled. I refuse to be a goddamn hostage in my own city. Ward, I want you by my side at all times that day.

R.E. Liles Sr.

From: WCrenshaw@RLIndustries.com
To: LilesRE@RLIndustries.com
CC: JSWard@RLIndutries.com
Subject: Re. Reunion part two
Date: June 12, 1996, 1:02 p.m.

Gentlemen, all security protocols have been put in place at the high school. I've also had our security department run extensive background checks on all the attendees, janitors, caterers, musicians and valets.

Everyone comes back relatively clean and all their whereabouts for the past five years have been well-documented by our system.

Sincerely,
Wadsworth Crenshaw

—

From the security audio tape of RL Industries at the New Harbor High School on June 22, 1996 at 7:20 p.m.:

Base 1: *"There seems to be a problem with some of the portable cameras in the gym. Mobile two, please check them."*
Mobile 2: *"Roger that, Base."*
Mobile 3: *"Base, this is Mobile 3. There seems to be something wrong with the sprinkler system. The pipes are making a noise."*
Base 1: *"Mobile 8, check the sprinkler system. Make sure no one has triggered anything."*
Mobile 8: *"Roger that, Base."*
Unknown Unit: *"EVACUATE! THE SPRINKLERS..."*
Screams from the crowd drown out the rest of the transmission.
Base 1: *"What's going on? Get Senior to the roof exit. Stay away from ground level exits! EVACUATE NOW!"*

Patience

Garbled transmissions and screams fill the radio broadcast.

—

New Harbor Ledger June 24, 1996

253 Dead in High School Mass Murder
By Jodi Muellar

NEW HABOR – In what is being considered one of the largest, single attacks on one generation of people in the United States, all 253 attendees of the Class of 1986 reunion were killed along with their spouses, guest speaker R.E. Liles, Sr., security officers, caterers and the band.

It appears that a "homegrown" terrorist replaced the water in the school's sprinkler system with a mixture of hydrogen cyanide, ammonia and an as yet undetermined acid compound. The chemical agent was released by a remote detonation device found in the sprinkler control room by federal agents.

The community of New Harbor is in a state of shock and mourning. A memorial is being held at 12:00 noon on July 1 at New Harbor City Park.

—

```
MILNET CIPHER
PAGE ONE OF ONE
TELEMAIL CODE 525151-33-51/30 JUNE 1996 0001 HRS
Al: TOPSECRET/SPECIALINTEL/BLACKOPS/ALPHA-023
FROM: XXX/XXX/WASHINGTON D.C
```

Sir,

Operation "Pascal" in Virginia was a success with minimal collateral damage. All advanced technology is now under our control. All operatives have been debriefed and the OPSPEC manual is being couriered to your office.

```
END MILNET CIPHER
READ AND DESTROY
```

—

```
LOGIN: GOLDSTEIN
PASSWORD: XXXXXXXXXX
WELCOME TO THE CRAY T3D
INIT: SOMA
SOMA STARTED
SYSTEM FAILURE IN 60... 59... 58...
LOGOUT
```

—

The Washington Post, July 4, 1996

Letter to the Editor

Welcome to the new world, a world that will not be taken over by computers and the people who operate them. No longer will the privacy of the human race be spied upon by government controllers.

This revolution happened with a keystroke in silence. You may not fully understand the gift I have given you, but someday you will, and on that day, you will thank me. You are now free to do what you want with your lives without the interference of a giant company or government monitoring every breath you take, and every penny you spend.

Have a good life, and as I say goodbye, I leave you with a quote from one of our founding fathers.

"I would rather be exposed to the inconveniences attending too much liberty than to those attending too small a degree of it." - Thomas Jefferson

Patience

Epilogue

New Harbor Ledger, July 31, 1996

Mysterious Findings
By Jodi Muellar

NEW HARBOR – With the growing reliance of DNA testing by our judicial system, it is fascinating to learn that, while many convictions have been affirmed, a large number of defendants have, in fact, been wrongly convicted. Then there is the use of DNA to identify remains at crimes scenes. And that is the case in this story.

Recent DNA testing of the remains from the 1986 fire located at 601 Aspen Road have concluded both bodies were male but not related. DNA testing proved one of the bodies was Deputy Randolph Fitzgerald, but the DNA from the second body did not have any genetic markers that showed any relationship between the two victims.

The Virginia State Crime Lab is attempting to match the second set of DNA from the fire scene to the DNA records on file. They have also contacted the FBI and requested assistance in trying to locate Mr. Edward Fitzgerald, the son of Deputy Randolph Fitzgerald, who has not been seen or heard from in over ten years.

If you know of Edward Fitzgerald's whereabouts, have seen him or heard from him, please contact Sheriff Brian Skelton of the New Harbor Sheriff's Department.

Birth of a Valkyrie
Fox Emm

The world has always been a cold, unforgiving place. It has never been fair or known to play by the rules. People have learned to live with it, mostly. The belief in karma, and that bad things would circle back and hit bad people when they earned it, kept most folk in line, but occasionally that frail belief would be insufficient to keep someone at bay. Those were the occasions when revenge needed to be delivered, but those times were few and far between.

Dinah Gunderson was a good girl, and a great student. She got into college without much of a fight. Her good grades and sufficient participation in extracurricular and volunteer activities during high school had allowed her to soar to the top of the admissions list. The mousy, studious young woman chose physics as her major once she was accepted, and gave little thought to the fact that she was one of only a few women in the department. She knew she deserved to be there.

Once she got involved in her coursework, things got harder. Merit-based scholarships and honors programs passed her by left and right. While working on a research project with the head of the department, Dr. Gregory Estivan, she noticed that her academic standing wasn't sufficient enough to keep propelling her upward. Despite her commitment to the faculty and staff, her high grade point average, and her willingness to always go the extra mile to achieve success, she was still not being chosen for leadership roles. Each time she was denied, she inevitably looked to see who won. Time and again she found that inferior males were being given opportunities to represent their laboratory at conferences and trade shows. Things began to look up when, near the end of the first semester of her second year, she learned about another such opportunity. She hoped her supervisors had been holding out on promoting her because they knew this was coming up, and this was a far greater honor.

When Dinah saw she finally had a response to her application, her heart raced. The palms of her hands and the back of her neck felt damp. She deeply inhaled and held her breath for a few moments before she let the air slip out in a slow, deliberate exhale. She double-clicked to open the email, but held her eyes skyward.

Please, she thought. *This is all I want.*

When she lowered her gaze to read the email's content, she breathed in sharp gasps, as though she had been punched in the gut. Heat rushed over her cheeks as hot tears welled in her eyes.

'We're sorry,' the email read, 'but we have selected someone else for the position. We thank you for your interest and wish you the best. We encourage you to apply for future opportunities within our department.'

"How is that possible?" she asked aloud. Her voice was just a notch above silent. "I have the best grades. I have the most experience. I was on debate and forensics, so it's not a matter of my ability to speak under pressure or in front of crowds." She scrolled down to the department's newsletter. Though the photo of the person selected wouldn't appear until the following week, the name was already included.

Him? This was the final straw. How could she be passed over for this promotion? It was the group *she* had founded to research *her idea*. Putting David in charge of the team was a slap in the face. He was only getting the role because he was the loudest during meetings and study sessions, but aside from stupid questions, he contributed little, if anything. What made things worse was that he would now get paid more than she did to participate in the discussions or do shifts of data collecting or processing.

She was dumbfounded. She drafted an email immediately to Dr. Estivan and to her faculty advisor, Dr. Larson.

By the end of the day, her email hadn't gotten a response and she was so angry she thought she might cry.

"How can they do this?" she hissed, her voice cracking as she spoke. "It's my idea. My group. My project."

She called Dr. Larson, who had been the source of a great many platitudes for losses of positions before. He didn't answer, and neither did Dr. Estivan. She tried to convince herself that she wasn't being ignored, that they weren't in the office, but she couldn't shake the feeling that they were dodging her.

After a few days of waiting, and several calls which went unanswered, she turned to the only person she had been able to trust: her father. He had always been a source of comfort and solid advice.

"Hello?"

"Hey, Daddy. How are things at home?"

"Quiet, as usual. I went over to clear off your mother's grave yesterday. How are you doing?"

"Just awful. No one listens to me here. I was just skipped for a promotion that would have made a huge difference on my resume, and there's nothing I can say. When I mentioned it to my advisor, who we're working with, he gave me some nonsense about how David is more qualified because he has leadership experience… I don't call being a team leader at Chuck-E-Cheese relevant experience, Dad."

"You'll figure out a way to make them listen. You've always been great at getting your point across, Pumpkin. You'll make them hear you. You're creative and smart – they'll have to listen."

His words were intended as a pep talk, for her to try things like giving a presentation rather than a speech, using real world examples, or, at the most dramatic end of the spectrum, staging a peaceful protest. He certainly wasn't condoning acts of violence. Unfortunately, much of life revolves around the interpretation of words rather than their intended meaning, incorrect or not.

*

The following afternoon, Dinah ran through the list of offenses against her and other women in her department. There were many, from outright sexual harassment and catcalling, to men telling them they "needed to smile" after going through a difficult break-up or losing a family member. There were no women in positions of power, either. Even the sole female faculty member was an associate professor who was at least a decade from tenure, assuming she got it at all. The sins committed against them were astonishingly numerous, and the greatest of all was simultaneously brazen and subtle: not a single woman was the head of a research group or project. Each new description of an incident or revelation that committed, studious women had been passed over made Dinah's blood boil and helped solidify her commitment to her plan.

She was willing to give the department one last try, however.

*

Dinah dropped by Dr. Larson's office the following morning and did her best to act as though she hadn't noticed him grimace upon sighting her. She wished she hadn't seen some of the color drain from his cheeks when she spoke his name, though. "Dr. Larson, hello. Do you have a moment?"

He nodded and gestured to the chair beside his desk. "Please, come in. How can I help you?"

"Thanks. I'm here about the—"

"The research position, right?" he said, not giving her time to launch into a speech she might have prepared for him. "I've been meaning to reply to your email. I've just been waiting on responses from the council members about their selection process."

Dinah sat in stunned silence. She hadn't expected him to interrupt her the way he had, and she certainly hadn't predicted he would claim there was a council involved in choosing an unqualified man over her.

She studied him for a few moments, waiting for elaboration. When none came she spoke again. "Well?"

"Well, what? I've been waiting for responses."

"What have you found out so far? I don't understand why David was chosen when I'm the one with the most research experience."

"He has the most professional knowledge. Right now, that seems to have put him ahead."

"Oh, okay. I didn't realize that it was essential to have worked outside the university when pursuing a purely academic position," Dinah said in an even tone, but the look she gave him and the words she chose made it clear she was unimpressed.

"I don't know what you want me to say, Miss Gunderson. The decision's been made."

"Okay," Dinah remarked. She nodded, trying to make herself okay with it by sheer force of will. "Well, thank you for your time."

*

Later that evening, Dinah, the pacifist, wrote letters to her father, the women in her department, and the school's administration. To her father, she apologized for not being strong enough to handle the situation better and reiterated that she loved him dearly. To the women, she explained that they were not the reason for her actions. Finally, her letter to the department was her manifesto. It explained what had been happening to her and the other ladies in great detail and offered suggestions for improvement. She made sure to mention the importance of having more women in power.

*

The following day, she skipped classes to gather supplies.

Semi-automatic handguns were easy enough to procure; they were practically lining the streets. She picked hers up in a nearby hunting shop. Since she was old enough to purchase a weapon, she had only needed to wait a few hours for the mandatory background check to return. (In her state, the obligatory waiting period had been reduced from forty-eight hours to eight.) She also acquired a sword, two machetes, three hunting knives, and a small camping hatchet. The shop clerk hadn't asked, but she made some excuse about an upcoming hunting trip with her father.

She laid the weapons and ammunition on her bed, and took a step back with her arms folded across her chest. She smiled broadly at the sight. The small arsenal looked a bit absurd, splayed out on the *Hello Kitty* comforter and sheet set she'd received for Christmas. It was a testament to the fact that she hadn't always been like this, though she didn't think of it that way. Prior to starting classes at the university, she had been given credit for her work and contributions. It was only after she'd been overlooked and hadn't been given equal compensation for her work that she had snapped.

Now, looking at the weapons she fully intended to use against those who had wronged her, she felt justified.

*

The morning of her attack she had a cup of coffee and some toast. She wanted to keep her energy levels high, her senses sharp, and her stomach settled (it would become soured by her anxiety otherwise).

She scrolled through her inbox and read her unanswered email about why she hadn't been chosen and began to lose patience once again. She would not back down or be ignored, not that day or ever again.

She snuck into the building which housed her lab, making sure no one was inside the room before bolting the door behind her. There she unloaded the weaponry from her duffle bag. She began transferring them to pockets and sheaths on her person but was interrupted by a knock at the door.

"Hey Dinah, are you in there?"

She gritted her teeth. "Yeah, David. I'll be there in a sec. The lock has been sticking this morning. You know how it gets sometimes," she called out to him in the friendliest tone she could manage. After unlocking it, she swung the door open and stepped behind it.

"Thanks! I figured if anyone was going to be here early on a Friday morning, it would be you. You're the most dedicated..." he began, but trailed off. "Hey, Dinah, are you just sitting in here in the dark?"

He didn't get the chance to turn and face her. He didn't get an answer to his question, either. She let the door swing closed and lock, which blanketed the room in darkness.

Before he could speak again or shout in alarm, she swung the hatchet and struck him hard in the back of the neck. He collapsed to the tile flooring like a ragdoll. She flipped on the light switch and hacked at his body with the sharpened side of her weapon.

Once David was lying in a growing pool of his own blood, she smiled before releasing a loud cackle. This was how she would get her revenge. One by one, person by person, sin by sin – they would all finally notice her (though it would be the last thing they ever did). She wiped the blade off on a dry spot on David's clothing before she reattached the hatchet to her waist.

Now the *real* fun could begin.

Dinah had memorized the Friday schedules for every person she intended to visit. She knew she could find her original academic advisor, Dr. Shook. The older man attempted to discourage her from pursuing a degree in hard sciences or mathematics. Why? *"Those fields are boys' clubs, and it will be harder for you there."* Dinah had always resented him for discouraging women from joining the sexist departments rather than disciplining the faculty and students who made them operate as such.

When she knocked on his open office door, he smiled and waved her in. She wore a long, flowing duster-style sweater which helped conceal her weapons.

"Miss Gunderson," he said, greeting her warmly. "To what do I owe the pleasure?"

"I had hoped you could help me plan my class schedule for next semester, Dr. Shook," she replied, forcing a sheepish smile. "My advisor is great at supervising research, but he isn't the best at helping me with the boring paperwork part."

"Absolutely, I can help. Though, since I'm not your advisor anymore, I can't look up your records. Would you mind signing me in?"

Dinah genuinely looked as if a wave of relief had washed over her. She widened her small smile into a grin. "Thank you so much! I want to be sure I graduate on time." She went around to the back of his desk and told the man her username and password for the scheduling program.

Once he'd signed on and clicked through a few screens to get to her upcoming class calendar, he paused. "Everything works on here as far as I can see. You seem to be on the right tra—"

She reached around and slit his throat with one of the long skinning knives. Blood squirted from his arteries and onto the computer and desk. He gurgled and sputtered before he tried to unsuccessfully hold his throat shut. After a brief period, he lost consciousness, but she stabbed him a few times for good measure. Since she had gotten him from behind, the only thing she had to be wary of when she left the room was stepping in the mess he had made.

She logged him off her username and powered the computer down before stepping around him. As she exited his office, she hung a small sign she had prepared on his door. It claimed he'd left early for a family emergency, but he'd be back Monday. That would buy her some time: housekeeping didn't work on Friday nights or over the weekend. By the time

Monday came around, she would be long gone.

She locked the door behind her, and continued down her short list. This time she was gunning for her actual advisor, Dr. Larson. The one who'd called her brilliant and had given the green light for her research, only to hand the most lucrative position to a man who joined in late and contributed nothing. No, she would not abide the blatant disrespect of giving away roles of power in her research group.

She knocked timidly on Dr. Larson's door. After a few moments and no answer, she tried again. She was worried that her mission might be compromised. What would she do if she couldn't punish the one who had committed the worst atrocity? Her anxiousness proved to be for nothing when she heard the man's familiar voice.

"Come in!"

She turned the knob and entered the small office. It looked like little more than a converted janitorial closet, but any room would have looked small with the giant of a man sitting behind the desk inside.

"Dinah, I didn't expect to see you again so soon. Come in and take a seat. I have to finish some paperwork for another student's graduation application, but I'll be done in a moment."

The young woman nodded and closed and locked the office door. Dr. Larson was oblivious to the fact that his door had been bolted. She could see the reflection of his screen in his glasses and pursed her lips. He wasn't filling out paperwork for a student – he was playing Solitaire.

Brilliant, she thought. *Glad to know I'm still not a priority.*

"So, what brings you in, Dinah?" he asked, not taking his eyes off the screen.

"I wanted to talk to you about David's promotion, again. You put him at the head of my project and I want to know why."

The man heaved a heavy sigh and rolled his eyes. He turned to face her for the first time, giving her his full attention.

"Look, Dinah, we've talked about this. He was promoted—"

"Because he has the most professional experience. I know what you said, but how about the truth this time?"

"I don't know what you're talking about."

"The best projects go on to compete at the state level, and at conferences around the nation. The leader of the research team is the one who gets to present at those competitions and conferences, and you didn't want to have a woman speaking for this department."

"That's absurd. I would love to have you participate. I only chose David because—"

Dinah raised a hand to silence him. "Because that summer he spent as a team leader-slash-bus boy at Chuck E. Cheese really prepared him for the management track, and you want to see him succeed. Am I close?" she hissed defensively. "Fine. If that's the lie you want to keep telling yourself, fine."

The man's eyes had diverted back to his game as she spoke, which only irritated her further.

"Can you at least help me clear something up about the experiment data? I think there was either a data collection or calculation error, but I'm unsure."

The man sighed but nodded. She moved around the desk as he logged into the mainframe.

"What am I looking for?" he asked.

"Check over the information for the last few days," Dinah instructed. "Tell me if you see anything weird."

As he scrolled, she drew the gun from its holster. She made sure the safety was off, and then pulled the hammer back.

Dr. Larson stopped reading at that sound. He was former military – he couldn't count the number of times he'd heard it. "Dinah? What are you doing?" he asked, raising his hands in his best 'don't shoot me' pose.

"I'm taking out the lying, cheating, misogynist, loser-promoting trash," she replied, pulling the trigger.

The bullet went through the back of his skull, leaving a small entry wound, but the .45 caliber round had torn a large section out of his face and took a good chunk of his nose along with it.

Blood splashed back on her from the impact and she smiled a 100-watt, all-teeth, prom queen smile. She kept on grinning as pieces of bone marrow and brain matter slid down the face of the broken monitor. She didn't dim her smirk even after she holstered her weapon and walked out of the small office.

They were remodeling the building next door, and she had conveniently decided to plan her revenge for a day that demolition was scheduled. The shot fired was assumed to be part of the jackhammering and controlled blasts outside, so no one came running.

Dinah's phone rang once she was outdoors and heading back for the lab. The caller ID let her know it was her father.

"Hey, Daddy," she crooned. *"What are you up to?"*

"Not a lot, Pumpkin. I wanted to call and see if you were having any luck getting through to the people at school."

"Much better. Actually, I don't think I'll have any more trouble with them. They're all seeing things my way."

"Good, girl. That's my baby. Well, I'll let you go. I'm sure you have some work to do."

"I do. I definitely do. Thanks for checking on me, Daddy."

"Anytime, Pumpkin."

When she got to the building she entered the lab through the back window she had climbed out of.

She stepped around the now sticky and drying blood which had pooled on the laminate flooring. She surveyed the grim scene for a moment before she turned on the nearest computer. There was no doubt she would be discovered soon, and she still had work to do. With no leadership left, it was a matter of time before their hard work was abandoned and forgotten. She had to finish the last round of edits on their manuscript before someone noticed all the blood. She didn't anticipate having more than an hour or two to work, but with any luck that was all she would need. She would not allow the day's sacrifices to be in vain.

The Hanging Wood
Guy N. Smith

Life was almost idyllic, Harvey Mitchell reflected as he set out with shotgun and Ellie, his springer spaniel, that foggy December afternoon. He had been appointed manager of a small rural branch of his bank only last year. A keen sportsman, the offers to shoot over several customers' farms were soon forthcoming, the latest being that owned by Frank Wylie. It comprised a few hundred acres, mostly grassland but with an oak wood on a steep hill amidst the fields.

Wylie had needed a loan to tide him over until he received his pending agricultural payment and Harvey had obliged. Hence he was here now on unfamiliar territory with maybe the chance of a shot or two and something to take home for the freezer. New ground was always exciting, as one never knew what it held.

"Heel!" he called the spaniel back, stood and surveyed those oaks which covered the hill up ahead. It would be a steep climb but it was the best place to flush a pheasant or two, maybe a woodcock. One never knew what to expect in such places.

Frank had told him that it was known locally as the Hanging Wood. It was rumoured that, after the sacking of a Roundhead stronghold in the Civil War by the Royalists, prisoners taken alive were hanged there. Harvey smiled to himself. Another local rumour of which there were many such throughout England. In effect there were numerous similar woods growing on steep ground named "hanging" woods simply because of their elevation. He pushed it from his mind and concentrated upon any game which he might find up there.

Dusk was already creeping across the landscape by the time he reached the fringe of that steep area. He wished that he had come here directly upon his arrival at the farm. Still, there should just be time to find a pheasant going up to roost or maybe a woodpigeon or two flighting in from feeding on the surrounding farmland.

"What the hell's up with you?" Ellie was hanging back, tail between her legs, clearly reluctant to enter that wood. She gave a low whine. That was very strange as usually he had problems keeping her close to him. "Come on, don't be so bloody stupid!"

She obeyed with obvious reluctance but, instead of walking to heel, she slunk some distance behind him with her belly close to the ground.

The hill was steeper than he had envisaged and the daylight was fading fast. Moss and lichen formed a slippery carpet beneath his feet and the giant oaks grew in weird, twisted shapes where the wind had battered them over the centuries. It would be tricky shooting any bird which flushed.

A hundred yards further on he paused for breath. As the daylight faded, a thin mist began to creep in.

"It's a waste of time today," he spoke to Ellie, who was still cringing behind him. "I think we'll head for home and give it a try another day."

There was an almost overpowering odour of rotting vegetation from the fallen leaves which carpeted the slippery, mossy ground, along with something else which penetrated his nostrils and throat. The stench of rotting flesh. It was probably from a decomposing fox or badger, he told himself, but somehow that did not seem quite right.

"Let's go home." He had half turned to retrace his slippery steps when he became aware of a rustling, low growing branches being thrust aside. It would not be from a small animal; perhaps it was a deer. Somehow that did not seem right. Whatever it was he wasn't going to hang around any longer. Ugh!

A sudden rasping cough was followed by a muffled mumbling which was definitely human. Somebody was coming downhill in his direction. Harvey experienced a desire to flee, which was just damned stupid, he told himself. Folks came up here, ramblers visiting the area. But surely not in this weather or at this time of day. The breeze which was bringing in the mist moaned softly. Like it was warning him. *Don't be so bloody stupid* he told himself.

"Come on, Ellie. The sooner we're out of here, the better."

Then a shape materialised out of the gloom. He saw an outline, upraised arms pushing obstructing branches aside, small twigs cracking. Whoever it was they were hurrying, probably eager to reach open terrain like himself.

"Who's there?" he spoke in a grating whisper.

The stranger came into view and paused a few yards in front of him, head thrust forward on stooped shoulders. The other's clothing was ragged, a jacket that hung in shreds, a near skeletal hand clutching a stick to support his frail, bent body. A whiskered face, pallid, with staring eyes that seemed to recede into their sockets.

"Go back!" the stranger spoke, his cracked tones barely audible. "Before it's too late. They are coming!"

"Who?" Harvey instinctively pushed the safety catch forward on his 12-bore, half raised the gun. "Who's coming? What's going on?"

The stranger halted. His breath was rasping as he held on to a tree trunk for support. There was something decidedly strange about his clothing, a long ripped and flapping coat that might have come from a long past era. A forest worker? A farmhand looking for missing livestock in this eerie wood?

"Flee, or else they will hang you like they've hanged the others!"

The guy was crazy. All the same, Harvey wasn't going to stick around any longer. There was no sign of Ellie for she had fled in terror. He turned away and that was when his foot caught a protruding tree root, flinging him headlong.

He cursed, dragged himself up into a sitting position. Now there was no sign of the mysterious stranger; he had vanished without a sound just like he had never existed. And that was when Harvey Mitchell heard more crashing through the wood up above, angry voices shouting. Whoever they were, they were heading in his direction.

He stumbled upright, raised his shotgun. Whatever was happening was crazy. He did not understand it and it was very frightening.

Human shapes materialized out of the deepening gloom. There were three of them, men in broad brimmed hats and long flapping coats, wielding what looked like broad-bladed swords. It had to be some kind of terrifying nightmare.

"Get the Revolutionist pig!" A hoarse shout rang out and the trio broke into a stumbling run.

Harvey gave way to panic. Even so he could not murder fellow humans in cold blood, and the double shot from his gun was directed over their heads, crashing reports in the stillness of the forest. A warning to them that he was armed.

It did not halt the oncoming trio. They were upon him in a rush, strong icy cold hands grabbing and holding him. The shotgun was wrested from his grasp, tossed aside, and now he faced his assailants.

Jesus God! Deathly white faces beneath those broad-brimmed hats, their expressions sheer hatred and unspeakable evil, their mouths slobbering. Their breath was foul and overpowering, had bile scorching his throat.

"Let go of me!" He screamed and a hand slapped his face.

"Traitor! Where is your companion?"

"I don't have a…"

A blow from a near skeletal fist and then icy, bony fingers gripped his throat. His arms were pinioned behind his back.

"Liar! Traitor to the King!"

It had to be a nightmare. Or else he had come upon a gang of poachers, criminals who feared recognition and arrest.

Their breath was rancid and that stench of decaying flesh was stronger than before.

"You will hang along with the others who sacked and sought refuge in Packington Hall. Traitors, all of you! God save our King."

Harvey did not understand. This was too crazy to be real. Strong, cold hands propelled him uphill, low growing branches whipping his face.

"The uprising will be put down. All traitors will hang!"

It was crazy, no way could it be real. They dragged him through a clearing where the fading daylight revealed a twisted oak. Something dangled from one of the lower branches, swinging gently to and fro. A body, a human corpse which had kicked its last vestige of life only minutes ago.

"Scum!" A hand slapped Harvey Mitchell's face. "You, too, will die along with those who rallied to Cromwell's call!"

His feet were dragged over the rough, steep terrain and his arms, twisted tight behind his back, threatened to snap under the strain. His brain spun, refused to accept that which was happening to him. He regretted shooting over the heads of those who now pulled him along; he should have blasted them into eternity and sod the consequences. Anything was preferable to this.

A second body dangled from a branch, still alive and choking its last, a ragged figure beneath which a long-bladed sword lay on the mossy ground. A third swung gently, a corpse in tattered garb which was soaked in blood. And further on yet another, barely discernible in the shadows of the approaching night.

"A rope," one of Harvey's captors grunted to the other two. "Fetch a rope!"

The hands which held him loosened their grip and he collapsed in a heap on the ground. A booted foot kicked him in the ribs, brought a gasp of pain from his dry mouth, which was greeted with coarse laughter from his captors.

"You will hang along with these others who defied the army of the king. Your uprising will result in many more deaths before it is defeated. Long live the king!"

All this could not be happening, it was impossible, he tried to convince himself. In an inexplicable return to the Civil War years, the Hanging Wood had become a scene of violent death.

Their companion had been gone some time and those guarding Harvey were becoming impatient, chiding their captive as they waited.

"The police will arrest you for murder." His threat sounded trite in this unreal situation.

"Police?" One man glanced, puzzled, at his companion. "What are police?"

Neither understood because they had somehow returned from the days when the law was enforced by soldiers of the king. It was all beyond Harvey's comprehension. It was impossible. He closed his eyes and prayed that it would all just disappear, that he would wake up and everything would be normal.

Footsteps heralded the return of the third Royalist, a giant of a man forcing his way through the undergrowth. A length of thick rope trailed in his wake.

"String him up," he grunted in command. "Hang him in the name of the King."

"No!" Harvey tried to shout but his plea came out as a hoarse whisper.

Two of the men pulled him roughly to his feet. The one with the rope slipped the noose over their prisoner's head, tugged it tight around his neck. Nothing would stop them now.

The end of the rope was tossed over a stout branch and then pulled taut. Harvey began to choke and there was no mistaking the taunts of the trio; they were enjoying every moment of this latest execution. One of them went to help their companion who was already starting to tug the length of frayed hemp. Another adjusted the noose around their prisoner's neck. All was ready for yet another death.

Harvey was mouthing final pleas for mercy. They were ignored. Now the trio began to take the strain, knees bent and heaving with all their strength.

That was when Harvey Mitchell fainted into blissful oblivion.

*

Harvey stirred. Something warm and wet was smoothing over his face. He began to regain consciousness. He groaned aloud, a hand supporting his neck, doubtless fumbling for the noose which would otherwise be strangling the life out of him. It was not there, just the collar of his thick shirt and a tie which was being loosened. He did not understand what was happening,

"Ellie!"

He found himself looking into the spaniel's face, her tongue continuing to lick his cheeks. Then he heard a human voice, one that he recognized instantly, and called out a name in sheer relief.

"Frank!"

It was Frank Wylie who was bending over him, torch in hand, a puzzled and worried expression on his florid features.

"Mister Mitchell, thank God you're all right. Your dog came down to the farm and there was no mistaking her insistence that I followed her up here. I guessed that something had happened to you. No broken bones, that's a relief," he said, running his hands over the bank manager's limbs. "I guess you must've had a fall, knocked yourself unconscious. Your gun's lying here. Both barrels have been fired. I heard the shots, thought maybe you'd fired at a pheasant or a pigeon going up to roost. How d'you feel now? Can you make it back to the farm with my help?"

"I'm okay, surprisingly." Harvey struggled up on to his feet with the other's help. "Let's get back into the warm and I'll tell you all about it. Maybe you can shed some light on what happened to me."

*

"That's how it was." Harvey drained the last of the mug of hot tea, felt his frozen body beginning to thaw out. "I can't explain it and I don't expect you to believe me. Shall we say I fainted and had a nightmare whilst I lay there?"

"I believe you, Mister Mitchell." Frank Wylie finished lighting his pipe, blew a cloud of smoke up to the ceiling. "There are various legends passed down through the generations of local folk, stories about Cavaliers hanging Roundheads up there in that wood on the hill after they had taken back Packington Hall. My folks once told me that my grandfather had a similar experience to yours. Ran for his life and managed to escape his pursuers by the skin of his teeth. None of the locals will go anywhere near the Hanging Wood after dark. Even these days some claim to have heard screams coming from up there."

Harvey's shiver had nothing to do with the cold that still lingered in his body. "I can't explain what happened to me but it was very real at the time. I'll have nightmares about it for years to come. That Hanging Wood is more than just trees growing on a hill. It's an evil place, take it from me."

"I wouldn't go up there myself after dark," the farmer admitted. "Not that I've seen or heard anything out of the ordinary at any time but I just wouldn't risk it. Following your dog was bad enough but I knew I had to find you. Thank God that I did. Tell you what, come Spring me and my workers are going to fell that wood, cut the trees up for logs and burn 'em. That way, whoever you saw up there tonight, if they exist, won't have any trees to hang anybody on. The Hanging Wood will be gone forever, maybe even forgotten in years to come. It's an evil place, take it from me!"

Carnage
Rose Garnett

Marnie knew there were three men following her as she walked down the rain-slicked pavement in the early hours of Saturday morning. The *tap, tap, tap* of her high heels echoed around the deserted street. A muffled snigger from one of the trio and she increased her pace, cursing the red stilettos that had seemed a good idea five hours ago in the safety of her flat.

She had been out on the hunt tonight, but hadn't met any decent candidates – and now, here she was, playing the part of someone else's prey. She pulled at her short, ruffled skirt, as though it would magically stretch to cover long, tanned legs. If she could get to her flat and the security of her pack, everything would be okay. Marsha had warned her not to get separated from the others as they worked the bars and, once again, she'd paid no attention. Everyone knew bad things happened to girls who didn't listen; it was the way of the world. She had put herself in harm's way once too often and now her luck had run out.

Marnie was about level with the entrance to the Meadows, a park she would normally cross as a quick route home. But now, chancing a swift glance behind her, she knew that was out of the question – she should stick to the comparatively bright main street.

They were gaining on her.

"It's got a sizeable arse on it, I'll give it that," one of them shouted.

"Room for two on that, at least," said another, higher voice.

From the cat-calls and laughter, she judged they were young, all wearing a uniform of tracksuit bottoms and oversized parkas, hoods up, hiding their faces. It was such a muggy summer night despite the earlier rain that the coats stood out as an odd choice – were they concealing weapons?

Scanning the street in front of her, there wasn't a soul in

sight. But then she realised her error as two more parka-clad men appeared from a side street, arms outspread as though in welcome. She calculated the odds of crossing the road – it was no use, she'd never make it. Whipping round in the direction of the park, she had no choice.

"Christ, she's gagging for it, this one," someone said.

As she made a run for it into the dark, tree-lined depths of the park, she realised they had been herding her in that direction all along. There was no CCTV in the Meadows and the good citizens of Edinburgh avoided the place after the sun set if they knew what was good for them.

Kicking off her shoes and dropping her bag, she sprinted down Middle Meadow Walk, intent on keeping to the path and making it across the common before they caught up with her.

Don't stray from the path.

Refusing to think about what would happen even if she did make it to the road on the other side, she ran as fast as she could, oblivious to the pain in her already bleeding feet.

It took her precious seconds to grasp there were no sounds of pursuit and she soon found out why.

As though at a pre-arranged signal, a horde of silent figures in parkas stepped out of the gloom and into the meagre light of the few old-fashioned streetlamps that lined the path.

What the fuck is going on?

Someone stepped out in front of her and she collided with them, falling to the ground, grazing her knees.

"What do you want?" she screamed.

"What do you want," someone mimicked in a high falsetto.

A beat of silence. A breeze, bringing with it the scent of newly mown grass, ruffled the cherry blossom in the trees and dappled the dim orange glow of the streetlights. From far off, she could hear the occasional rumble of lorries as they motored by, oblivious to her plight.

She was yanked to her feet by her long hair and dragged, kicking and protesting, deep into a darkened grassy area. Thrown onto the ground, she struggled to stand, but was pushed back down by insistent hands. The crowd fanned out around her, forming a circle of hooded, jeering figures.

Christ, there must be hundreds of them.

An expectant hush was broken by a large, burly man who strode up to her and punched her, hard, in the face. *Crack*, a warm rush of blood – her nose was broken.

"Please, tell me what you want. I've got money – it's yours – just let me go," she gabbled through blood and snot.

The burly man took his hood down and shone a torch under his jowly, bearded face. Thin grey hair struggled to make it past pock-marked cheeks. "It's *you* we want, don't we, boys?"

"Oi, what about us?" shouted an unseen woman.

"You women's libbers, what are you like?" The big man rolled his eyes and grinned, revealing brown, rat-like teeth.

"Who are you?" quavered Marnie.

Some of the mob pretended to sob and someone threw a large stone that thunked her on the forehead – she reeled, almost passing out.

Even if, by some miracle, she escaped this horror, Marsha would kill her for breaking one of the cardinal pack rules – getting caught by humans. If they found out what she was…

"I'm Brother Brian, and I'll be your attacker for tonight," said the big man to hoots of laughter, holding a hand over his heart. "That's me, but who are we collectively though, that's the more interesting question, isn't it, ladies and gents?"

A roar of approval went up from the assembled crowd.

"Please," Marnie sobbed, "just let me go. I won't tell anyone, I promise!"

"You're not really getting this, are you? Okay, here's what I'll do for you. Before we, eh, have a go, as it were – and since you've asked – I'm going to tell you about the new setup. Don't say I'm not good to you," he said, switching the torch off.

A soft groan to her left – Marnie turned towards it. In the distance, a police siren faded into nothing.

"Show her what we've made," yelled a voice.

"Now, we don't want to scare the poor little thing to death, do we?" said Brother Brian. "Not before we get what we came for, surely?"

"Show her, show her, show her," chanted the mob.

"Oh, alright, can't hurt – take her over to say hello. I'm just a big softy, me," said Brother Brian, gurning as he kicked what looked like a large sack, once, twice, three times. Whatever was imprisoned inside screamed, high and shrill, before breaking down into a hopeless sobbing.

Marnie was seized and hauled over to where the noise had come from. A dark mound towered in front of her, as though someone had built a huge bonfire and forgotten to light it.

"She can't see it – where's the fun in that?" a guttural voice rasped.

Brian sighed. "You don't deserve me, you really don't," he said, switching the torch back on.

"Don't do that – someone'll see," shouted a young man, rushing forward, ginger dreads and waist-length beard flying.

"Fuck that, Brother Simon. Our days of skulking in dark corners are over – or haven't you been paying attention?" roared Brother Brian, voice rising as he stabbed the air for emphasis. "Besides, we're too far in – aren't we, boys and girls?"

A crescendo of whoops and wolf-whistles greeted his words.

"Alright, you dirty buggers, calm down," Brother Brian continued. "There's time for that after we've given our guest the guided tour."

The fact that these lunatics weren't bothering to conceal their identities now she had been captured was the latest in a road trip of bad signs that led nowhere she wanted to go.

I wouldn't be here now if I'd listened to Marsha.

She didn't follow the thin beam of light as it played over the mound, but Brother Simon grabbed hold of her and forced her head round.

"If you don't open your eyes, we'll cut off your eye-lids,"

he told her in a posh, Morningside accent.

"That's my boy," shouted a woman from the crowd.

"That's not what you said last night, you filthy bitch," said another, to the raucous laughter of the mob.

But Marnie scarcely heard as she tracked the torch in its progress. The beam lingered on a bloodied head rammed onto a stick, mouth agape and stuffed with tender, fleshy parts, one eye a glistening, red ruin. Then a dismembered arm, a glint of bone protruding from the shoulder joint. More limbs than she could count; a detached breast, coated with blood and thicker matter, decorated with the imprint of human teeth where the nipple should have been. A male torso, with pride of place on top of the pile, words carved into the flesh of the stomach in jagged, bloody letters.

"Can you read that, bitch?" hissed Brother Simon into her ear as she struggled to be free of him, the goaty reek of his beard almost making her vomit. "No? Well, I'll tell you," he continued. "It says '*Take Back The Night*'. Do you know what that means?" he screamed, spitting into her face. "Do you? You bitches used too moan about it often enough. Well, you're playing by our rules now, slut – and guess what, we win."

Marnie wasn't listening. Everything was in slow motion as it hit home that the mound in front of her was a pile of dead bodies – one she was clearly supposed to join.

I've died and gone to hell.

A groan from the pile.

Someone lit a row of homemade torches: large planks of wood, crowned with cloth, stuck into the ground. Flames crackled and danced, birthing flickering shadows that played over the mutilated corpses.

"You fuckers couldn't break a fucking taboo if you had it bent over your knees, arse up," yelled a fat woman, pounding over to the corpses and throwing body parts around like skittles. "Right – where are you, you bastard?"

Brother Simon released Marnie, but she was rooted to the spot, paralysed.

"If you're going to kill me, get it over with," she said, all hope seeping from her.

The fat woman had found the groaner, a slight adolescent of indeterminate sex. Casting around for a weapon, she picked up a large stone, already slick and dark with a substance that looked like blood. Hefting it in her hand like an expert, she began to pound the head of the juvenile, the wet crunch of bone finally giving way to a watery slapping as the skull shattered.

"That'll learn ya, you little fuck," she screeched, burying her head in the youngster's naked belly, biting through the flesh, her long unbound hair falling forward into the uncovered intestines.

But the youth still wasn't dead, a soft *phlppph* issuing from the ruin that had been its face as the woman guzzled down bloody chunks of its internal organs. An acrid stench drenched the warm air, and Marnie guessed the youngster's bowel had been pierced.

"Oh, we're not getting anything over anytime soon, my impatient little pussy cat," said Brother Brian to screams of mirth. "I still haven't told you who we are," he said, torch again ensconced under his chin.

"I don't give a fuck," said Marnie, offering the only resistance she could, aware it was futile.

"Well, that's too bad, because we do," whined Brother Simon.

"As the words carved into that cop's chest say, we're taking back the night and there's nothing you or the moral majority can do about it," said Brother Brian, pulling something fleshy from the pile of body parts and taking an enormous bite.

Marnie struggled against instantaneous nausea. "What are you talking about? You'll never get away with this – you're all crazy," she screamed.

Hands closed around her, hauling her up and onto an impromptu cross. Her arms and legs were tied crucifixion style.

The pain was excruciating as her arms took the strain of her entire weight.

Meanwhile, below her, the fat woman and some others arranged kindling around the base of the cross, singing 'Whistle While You Work'.

Wait, isn't this like that terrible film – what was it – The Surge or something?

"If you think you can get away with a night of chaos, you're wrong, you bastards," she shouted with her last reserves. Her weight bowed her arms further – any minute they'd be free from the life-long tyranny of their own sockets.

Brother Simon sniggered, a line of snot falling onto his ginger beard. "She thinks this is about one night of freedom."

The expanding crowd laughed and whistled in response.

"Well, it's not," he continued, whipping round to point a shaking finger at her. "It's the rest of our lives."

"Aye, okay lad," said Brother Brian, tone paternal. "Okay. The bitch has it wrong. Is that not ever the way though?" he appealed to the crowd, arms wide.

They roared their approbation.

"Don't worry though," Brother Brian continued. "She's still got her very own fry-up to enjoy. Then we'll see how gobby she is."

He went over to where she hung, her clothes in shreds, a line of piss leaking down into the assembled garbage at the bottom of the cross. "It's not one night, whore. It's all of them. Do you still not understand?"

Hoping this would delay the moment where she was set alight, she shook her head, the effort almost beyond her.

"They have names for people like us: perverts, paedophiles, murderers, rapists, arsonists, peeping toms, cannibals, predators, sexual fetishists, sadists – sinners all, or so we're told. They tell us we're criminals – the dregs of society – and that's without having the slightest understanding of a way of life that demands qualities the rest of the drones can't even comprehend, never mind have. I'm talking about free-thinking, ingenuity, passion, *commitment*."

Guy N. Smith

Brother Brian spat out the words like bullets, one hand hammering the palm of the other for emphasis. "That may be so, but we're everywhere and we've had e-fucking-nough of being made to feel like we've got something to be ashamed of. We've been infiltrating your kind for years – we're your doctors, lawyers, surgeons, prison officers, brickies, factory workers, civil servants, your world fucking leaders, and we've penetrated every last inch of this so-called moral society.

"You haven't been able to get rid of us or jail us all, whatever new-thought crime strategy you've come up with. But most importantly, you can't defeat us if we stand together. And, oh, we do stand together, my friends, don't we?"

The crowd was transfixed, all eyes on the orator.

"And this isn't just for a night or a week or a month – it's from now on. Despite our persecution, we have endured and become stronger. And now – we are fucking legion!" bellowed Brother Brian, beating his chest.

The instantaneous, mighty roar from those assembled made Marnie close her eyes. A twin track of tears ran down both cheeks.

What have I done to deserve this?

"And we've had enough," he continued.

Marnie groaned, praying for a quick death that refused to come.

"Well, the straights have had their chance and screwed things up good and proper. We live in a world where you're not allowed to so much as sniff your own farts without some nosy, interfering bastard popping up to tap you on the shoulder, telling you what you can and can't do. But now it's our turn to come out of the closet, into the light and take up the reins of power that are rightfully ours. Our time has come, brothers and sisters, it has come!"

The crowd howled and cheered its approval.

Then, out of the night, a hooded figure hurled itself on Brother Brian.

"What the fuck?" he demanded, brandishing a knife at the

newcomer.

"Sorry, Mister," said the figure, taking down its hood to reveal the smooth pale face of a young boy of around eight or nine. "My name's Brother Steven, and I've been sent by Brother Isaac to tell you there's a mass gangbang on the south side. There must be fifteen of them – the crowd are going nuts. Brother Isaac says to come now or they won't last what's being done to them. They've got blowtorches and everything. It's so cool!" The boy's eyes shone in the reflected light of the torches, his thin body quivering with excitement.

"Boys or girls, Brother Steven?" asked Brother Brian, stroking his beard.

"Boys *and* girls," said the child with obvious pride, as though talking about ice-cream flavours.

"We can't leave this little slag," moaned Brother Simon.

Brother Brian looked up at where Marnie hung and their eyes met. Pursing his mouth, he said, "Skinny bitch can keep – not enough of her to go round, truth be told. Too much cannibalism and too little hot sex action make Brother Brian a *very* dull boy. Let's go, brethren."

Marnie scarcely dared breathe.

"But someone might find and rescue her," Brother Simon persisted.

The big man eyed him and then his face cracked into a grin. "Haven't we just mounted a takeover? Half the cops in St Leonards are brothers now. I don't think there'll be any rescue anytime soon. Let's go and have some fun – whaddya say, brothers and sisters, eh? Quickly, before those south-siders get all the good stuff."

The crowd were incandescent now, shouting, whooping and screaming their ecstasy as they streamed off into the night.

In the eerie, sudden silence, she risked calling out, only too aware it might attract one of the monsters who had put her here.

"Please, help me. Help me," she croaked, but her voice was only a dry husk.

She must have passed out, because when she opened her eyes again, Marsha's thin, pinched face was looking up at her.

Please God, don't make this a mirage.

With Marsha were three of the girls from her pack, all dressed for a night out on the town, hair straightened, lips glossed, as though they'd just stepped out of a beauty salon.

Marsha tossed back her mane of long, black hair. "Did you think you'd get away with this?"

"What are you talking about? Get me down from here, Marsha."

"No."

"What do you mean, no? Get me down from this fucking cross – come on you guys, help me, please. I was attacked by a crazy mob and they may be back any minute."

"Then they'll find you, won't they?"

"Look, I don't have much strength left – get me down and take me back to the flat."

"No, Marnie – you've disobeyed the rules once too often. And now you've broken one of the most important: never get separated from the pack and hunt alone," said Marsha, examining long, manicured nails.

"I'm sorry," she continued, "but there's nothing I can do about it. We have to live by a code and if we don't, we're less than human or animal. You decided, in your wisdom, that the code you signed up for when you joined my pack didn't apply to you. Now you have to take the consequences. Goodbye, oath-breaker, and good riddance."

Marnie's four packmates stared up at her, expressionless, then turned on their heels and walked away, swallowed up by the night.

"Don't leave me, please. Don't leave," shrieked Marnie, convulsing against the rope so hard, the resulting spasms of pain caused her to pass out.

When she came to, she had no idea how much time had lapsed, her only companion the grinding pain that wracked her entire body. She was sure her arms had been pulled out their sockets.

The sky was lightening and, along with the birds, she could hear yells and shouts in the distance – the mob were returning. Having rescue offered and then snatched away was far worse than her physical agony.

Wait, what's that? Someone's nearby – is it them?

She tried and failed to turn her head, panicking. A young man with long, fair hair caked in blood limped into her line of vision.

"Please, don't hurt me," she muttered.

"I'm not one of those wankers – I'm here to help, not hurt you. I'll call your friends and they'll get you down from there – you're too high up for me to reach on my own. We're going to need to take the cross down, lay it flat and then untie you while you're on the ground. Who were those girls who spoke to you – why didn't they help? Fucking sight-seers make me sick."

The young man's clothes hung around him in rags and his arm was bent at a strange angle, suggesting it had been broken.

"Get an ambulance," moaned Marnie.

"We can't risk it. These lunatics are everywhere. Oh, and I'm Robert, by the way."

"Phone your friends then, Robert, because I no longer have any. Hold on." She closed her eyes, concentrating. "Why didn't you call your mates before, if you have a mobile?"

"Making phone calls isn't really an option when you're being savagely beaten. Besides, it would only have gotten them killed."

"Where did you come from?" said Marnie, suddenly suspicious of her white knight.

"I was attacked like you. They stuffed me in a sack and beat me – that total bastard Brian kept knocking the wind out of me. They caught me in Marchmont as I was on my way home and they've been torturing me ever since – they even carved stuff into my chest and back, can you fucking believe it? One of them tried to hack my foot off, but then they snatched you and I was saved. Just try to hang on 'til my friends come."

"Oh, I'm going to do a bit more than that," said Marnie.

"Oh, like what?"

"Those bastards pride themselves on breaking the rules, so I'm going to show them how it's done."

Robert's eyes flickered. "What?"

"Let's just say those sight-seers inspired me to break the number one prohibition of my pack: I'm going to transform in public for the whole world to see. And when I do, I'm going to kill them all – the mob, my pack, every last motherfucker."

"Your pack?" Robert said, uncertainty in his voice. "Please say you're not one of those nut-jobs that think they're a werewolf?"

"I'm so much worse than that," she snarled, curling her palms towards her wrists, her extending nails cutting into the rope that bound them.

The mob draws close. I must work faster.

"Hey, your skin has gone all… fuzzy," Robert said, dropping the phone as she succeeded in cutting one of her hands free. "And there's something wrong with your teeth…"

"You should fall to your knees in honour of this moment, fool," she growled, freeing the other hand as her now elongated feet slipped free of the rope. She dropped to the ground on all fours, tearing her clothes off to reveal a back rippling with a forest of spotted fur. The huge, striped head with the tufted ears and long muzzle was like a grotesque feline mask, a travesty of human and animal combined in an affront to the laws of evolution.

Robert froze, finally frightened.

"Please don't hurt me – I was trying to help you."

"Run," said Marnie, through a crowded mouth. "The mob approaches and I'm losing control. Run, and pray to God I don't catch you."

Don't Be A Cunt
(The Only Rule To Follow)
Toneye Eyenot

What a piece of shit world we live in, when one has to pay to wake up. Taxed from the moment you switch on a light because it's stupid o'clock in the fucking morning, it's still dark outside and will be for at least another hour-and-a-half, and you stumble around like a zombie to get ready for work.

Work. What the fuck is that about, anyway? I'll tell ya. It's about draggin' your arse outta bed five days a week, goin' to a place you hate bein' at and slavin' your guts out for eight hours a day to make some fat, greedy cunt rich off the sweat of your labours. And that's not even the worst part. Two days out of five you do it for free. That's right, fucking *free*! That's the percentage of your time and hard-earned pittance goin' to the *T*axman. (There's that dreaded 'T' word again.) Never thought about that, did ya? No, because all you can think about is makin' it to your next paycheck without snappin' and smashin' the boss's smug face through his mahogany desk. Isn't that just enough to make you say, *"Fuck this shit, I'm gonna start killin' cunts if this continues much longer"*?

You're a slave. Blundering your way around this free-range prison we call 'society' under the illusion that you're uncontrolled. But you're not. Don't fuckin' kid yourself, mate. None of us are. We're the bottom feeders, consuming the excrement of our 'betters', who in turn are consuming the excrement of their betters and so on and on, all the way up the shit-smeared ladder to *success* – a word only a select few ever truly manage to grasp the concept of. If achievement is measured by hard work and perseverance, then shouldn't we all be succeeding? By rights, yes, we should be, but we aren't. We're trapped in an endless cycle of 'sleep, wake up, work, consume, sleep, wake up, work, consume' until ya eventually get to retire with fuck-all time left to reap any significant reward for a life of toil.

All I can say is, thank fuck they abolished the carbon tax. Think about that for a moment. It's fine if you wanna inhale, but in order to carry on livin' you need to exhale, and to exhale they expect you to pay a tax for that? A tax to fucking breathe? Come on! How much more can they squeeze out of us before there's simply nothin' left?

Getting' to ya, aren't I? I can see that vein throb, the spastic twitch in your eye as I slowly drag you outta the fugue you've lived in your entire life. Those fucks who sit in their ivory towers, making up rules and laws to dictate how you live – the untouchables – laugh with abandon at the billions of performing monkeys under their control. I know you. You're a decent person and try to do right by everyone – a noble trait. What do ya get in return, though? Gratitude? Yeah, from some. Most, however, are caught up in their own mental miasma and overlook the efforts of their fellow man. Society has become so numb, so… selfish. It's not their fault. They're just like you: trying to get by in an increasingly hostile world.

But to protect themselves from being exposed, these secretive demons who pull our strings divert our attention from their nefarious doings and cast it onto others like yourself. Your hatred, your anger, your fucking furious rage, if combined with the frenzy of seven billion others, would bring those ivory towers crashing to the ground faster than the World Trade Centre. Divide and conquer; that's the age-old game they play. While you get shuffled around on the gameboard of life, obeying your invisible masters – teachers, the judicial system, law enforcement… fuckin' God – you have been taught to hate people you don't even know based on nothing more than a label. Religion, social status, political persuasion, you name it – they are nothing more than systems of control designed to keep you docile while you stuff your face on toxic garbage packaged as food and cheer for your favourite, grossly overpaid football team on the idiot box.

All the while, throughout these myriad of carefully

orchestrated distractions, those men in their ivory towers hatch foul plots against us.

That's it. Now you're gettin' it. I see that spark in your eye, now let it ignite. Know your enemy and don't let 'em tell ya what to fuckin' do anymore. This is your life, and yours alone, so live and die on your terms, not theirs. Fuck their rules, because the only rule which holds any validity is 'don't be a cunt'; everything else is tyranny and oppression, inflicted upon you by, yep… *cunts.*

PINNNNGGGG!

Welcome to your epiphany.

I'm glad you've finally understood and taken heed. I am your voice of reason, and let me tell you, after all these decades in your numb skull, watchin' you through your clouded eyes, bowin' to your masters and demandin' homage from your peers like a good little slave, there have been times I've wanted to walk you out into traffic, off a cliff, or into that woodchipper in the lumberyard you've slaved at for the past twenty-five years. Whichever method, ending your miserable existence would've been a pleasing respite because I don't think I could've taken much more of your blind ignorance. You are better than that.

So, are ya just gonna keep on sittin' here? Let's go! It's time to fight back. Time to fuck the system that's been fuckin' you nine ways from Sunday since ya left the womb. I know just the place to start. Where it all began with you: TV. This was where your indoctrination was initiated, where you were first exposed to the insidious art of distraction. Your parents weren't to know that when they plonked you down on the floor in front of the idiot box so you'd be quiet and out of the way, they were pluggin' you into the matrix. Your sledgehammer in the shed will take care of the immediate problem, and then we can move onto the bigger 'picture' – the local broadcasting station.

That's it, take a swing. *Wait!* Unplug it from the wall first, idiot. You wanna electrocute yourself? That'll bring things to an untimely end. Geez.

I have to prepare you for the fact that people are gonna die. It's a necessary evil, though. Don't feel bad. They have been complicit in dispensing the materials – the mind poison – which has helped keep you docile and subservient to a bullshit agenda. From the deceptively named *reality* shows which dominate television programming, interspersed with blatant as well as subliminal advertisements to make you feel you need things which are useless, to the worst of all: the *news* reports, so embellished of the truth and grossly sensationalised to evoke the desired emotional response. They have been brainwashing you your entire life. Fuck them. They are parasites and need to be eradicated.

You feel better, yeah? Feels good to destroy something that has ruled your life. Trust me, this is nothing compared to what you will feel when you are finally free. Tip of the iceberg right here.

It's one AM and the cleaner at the TV station will be finishing his shift in half an hour. You ready? Let's do this. You wanna arrive before he leaves, and it's gonna take at least fifteen minutes to get there. After that, you'll have about four hours to completely destroy the joint before the puppets turn up for the day's puppet show.

Grab your hoodie and a bandanna to wrap around your face. You'll be on camera … at least until ya take 'em out, hehe.

*

You're drivin' like an old bitch – put ya foot down, for fuck's sake. There's nobody on the road at this hour; fuck the speed limit. That's another bullshit rule. You're a competent driver. As long as you're safe, you can go as fast as ya damn well please. Red light? Run the cunt. It's early hours and there's nobody around to hit. Red – a colour known to promote irritability and increase rage. Why the fuck do they make a stoplight red? I don't give a fuck how they try to explain that one away or justify it. How many people enjoy coming to a stoplight? Fuckin' no one.

Here we are. Pull up over there, outta sight.

Now we wait. Yeah, sometimes when ya decide to fuck the rules, there's a little waitin' involved if ya wanna do it right. You timed it well, though. He should be comin' out in a few minutes. See? If you'd stuck to the limit and waited at that light, chances are you'd have turned up too late.

That must be his car over there. It's a pretty lit-up area of the car park. How's your throwin' arm? C'mon, let's do this. You have a few minutes, tops. Grab some rocks from around that garden and take out those lights, quick. May as well take 'em all out while you're at it. Plunge the whole exterior into darkness; it'll be harder for you to get spotted.

Nice! You're a fuckin' natural, mate.

Alright, gonna spring this one on ya so don't freak out and bail on me. You're gonna have to kill this cunt. Bein' your voice of reason, there's a good chance I'm gonna fade into your subconscious for a spell while logic takes a back seat. Shit's gonna get messy and more than a little chaotic, but I have faith in ya. You can do this. Just think of him as a TV set as ya bash his brains in.

I'm only sayin' this because you'll need his keys and the security code to get in without trippin' the alarm. Just break his leg at first. You're gonna need him to turn off the thing, and then fuck him; he'll have outgrown his usefulness. Kill the cunt, because if ya don't, he'll squeal and the pigs'll be here before ya get a chance to destroy much of anything. We've got a lot more to do after this.

Yeah, yeah, I know. 'Don't be a cunt'. Think of it this way: Y'know the saying, "*To make an omelette, ya gotta break a few eggs*"? Well, as rough as it might sound, this cleaner is just an egg and you have one helluva big omelette to make. Chalk it up to collateral damage and try not to think about it too hard. You've got this, mate.

Quick, hide! Here he comes. Remember, the crowbar will

probably kill him straight up if ya hit him in the head and we don't want that. Not yet, anyway. Just aim for the knee, but be prepared to shut him up real quick because that fucker is gonna scream like a bitch.

Don't chicken out on me now. Damn, your heart is beatin' fast! Stay with me, man. The blood poundin' in your ears is fuckin' loud. You'll wanna be able to hear what I'm sayin'. Just stay here behind the car until he gets to his door. Ready? *Ready*? OK, *now*!

Shut him the fuck up! He's gonna scream the whole fuckin' neighbourhood down. Shove that glove in his trap. That's the way. Ah shit, man, that even made me cringe. That's no easy feat either. Nicely done.

Time for Mr. Cleanerman to go back to work. Double shift for this fucker. Pick his keys up. You're gonna need that swipe card. Get him up, let's go. If he won't – or can't – walk, fuckin' drag him. Threaten to take out his other leg.

*

We're in, alarm is disarmed, now fuck him up. Just one to the h— OK , two. Or three… four.

He's dead, man. You can stop now. Fuck, mate. You like this a little too much. Remember, don't be a cunt. We're here to destroy this place and time's a-tickin'. Let's start with takin' out that camera. You're covered up pretty well but you never know these days. Don't forget your gloves. No fingerprints. Right, we have a few hours to play. Let's see how much damage you can do.

Ah, the TV production studio. So this is where the magic happens. Where they manipulate footage to suit whatever agenda they wish to push on the gullible population. Smash it all, room by room. A crowbar is such a versatile tool, don't ya think?

Nice work, mate. You're really gettin' the hang of this. You have a nice smile when you're enjoyin' yourself. You should enjoy yourself more often, hahaha. Leave it; you've done sufficient destruction here. There's so much more to see.

The studio floor: this is where the actors play their role. So much to see here, all of which is manufactured – fake. Start with their precious green screen. Destroy that shit, their treasured tool of deception. All these cameras, stage lighting rigs, video monitors – smash 'em and then we'll move on to the control room for the final blow.

Well, this'll be easy. Wait, do you smell smoke? Looks like you've started a fire back there in the studio. Well, well, well! Things just got even easier! Quick, into the Master Control Room for a speedy rampage – just for good measure – and then you're outta here. You can let the fire do the rest. I suspect fire alarms will be goin' off any minute now. Make sure you demolish that panel there good 'n' proper. That's the sprinkler system. Can't have that undoin' all your hard work now.

Poor ol' cleaner man will be burnt to a crisp; might even be charred beyond any sign of foul play on your part.

OK, let's get outta here.

*

Now, tell me that wasn't fun, yeah? Liberating, innit? Ah, don't feel bad for the egg. Your omelette is startin' to take form and you wanna be able to enjoy a good meal when this is all over.

Now I'm gonna let ya think for yourself. After all, this is what it's all about. So, you started out on the road to your enslavement as a very young boy, having the te*lie*vision slowly brainwash ya into subservience. What came next? School, yeah, but there was something before that. C'mon, think. Fuckin' hell, do I have to spell it out for ya? *Think!* I just gave you a clue right there. No, not spell; sounds like, though. Hell, good. And where do we get the rikokulous notion of this imaginary place? You guessed it, buddy: you're goin' to church, hahahahaha.

You probably don't remember this (it was such a long time ago), but when you were just a wee sprog, your parents took ya to one of these houses of lies and had some sick motherfucker try to drown ya in the name of his imaginary sky fairy. You might not recall, but I do. You were fuckin' terrified and traumatised. You screamed the fuckin' place down and for the next year afterwards, bath time was a nightmarish reliving of that fateful day. You do remember the years that followed, though. Earliest memories of Sunday mornings, goin' with Mum 'n' Dad back to that shithole to have the fear of God hammered into ya with nine-inch nails of bullshit.

It's not even four AM and Father *Fiddler* will still be asleep in his quarters. Make a quick stop home first. I have plans which will require the use of your Bowie knife. That's right, mate: you're about to break another egg. Might not use this one for your omelette though. This egg is rotten as fuck.

The streets are still empty, so why are ya doin' the speed limit? Man, you have some serious unlearnin' to do. Fuckin' step on it!

*

Holy Trinity Catholic Church: Would ya look at this joint! What a pretentious, elaborately designed monstrosity, and these cunts preach humility and frugality. Check out the BMW – wait. Fuck, he has two! All these shit-brained social commentators loudly blame the lower class no-hopers on welfare for bein' a burden on the economy. Here's the real burden. This is where a lot of your hard-stolen tax dollars go, while these cunts don't pay a single fucking cent to live in luxury and convince their idiot flock of sheep to give 'em even more money. Fuckin' parasites.

You can take care of his sweet rides after. Ya don't wanna alert him to your presence until you're hoverin' over his bed, blade in hand. Grab the crowbar – you'll need it to jimmy open his door.

*

Sleepin' like a baby. Look at the fat fuck. I bet he eats well every night. Give him a nice whack on the head with the crowbar, but don't kill him – not just yet.

Holy shit! Fucking disgraceful piece of human garbage! Is that a boy beside him? Man, I shouldn't be surprised, but this complicates matters somewhat. Even I feel bad about this, but you're gonna hafta take care of him. Tie the lad up, gag him and lock him in that closet. He doesn't need to see what's about to go down. Be careful not to hurt him. Remember: don't be a cunt. Poor kid. He probably has no idea that what he's been havin' done to him is despicable and wrong.

I know, you just wanna bash this fucker's brains to mush, but he has to suffer first. This is the lowest act of depravity I can think of, and people have no fucking idea what goes on in the privacy of his bed. I am almost inclined to stand back and watch you go to town on him, but let's be methodical about this, yeah? Cut the cunt's tongue out first. Ya don't want his screams to traumatise the kid more than he already is. Just rip it out of his mouth and slice – don't be gentle. This should rouse him from the light clobberin' ya just gave him.

Brilliant, he's awake. *Ha-ha!* Oh, that terror in his eyes is just divine, yeah? Drag him out onto the floor and grab that nice thick candle. Aw, how helpful he is. He's already naked. Piece of shit. Make him kneel, good. Now shove his face into the floor and ram that candle deep into his filthy arse. *Use the force, Luke*; he's got room in there.

I see you are enjoying yourself again. You're a sadistic fuck, aren't ya? Layin' the boot in to kick that candle up into his guts is a particularly savage touch, haha. Gotta say, I'm enjoying the show myself. He's gettin' what he deserves.

Boot him onto his back. There's one more thing you need to do to finish him off. That's the way. Now cut his fuckin' cock off. He won't be puttin' that where it don't belong anymore. A tongueless scream is a scream nonetheless. You've made some room in that filthy mouth of his, now stuff it with a dick fatter than he's used to takin' in there.

Nicely done, mate. Now burn this fuckin' house of depravity and lies to the ground and let's get the hell outta here. Grab the kid first and take him to the car park. He won't go anywhere bound like that.

A glorious sight, innit? A holy funeral pyre for a disgustingly unholy fuck. Good riddance, Father Fiddler. May you rot in your imaginary Hell.

*

OK, what's next? You're getting' the hang of this; time for you to think for yourself again. It'll be daylight soon, so where do ya wanna go now? What's another institution designed to enslave? Yes, you've got it: school. Thirteen years of indoctrination into a system where you are taught, above any academic learning, to be obedient and follow an insane amount of ludicrous rules. They want you smart enough to be a productive worker and stupid enough to swallow the bullshit they force down your throats without ever questioning their authority. In many ways, the education system is far more insidious than organised religion.

You seem to have developed a pattern here. I think arson at the local public school is in order. Burn it to ashes before the day of indoctrination begins for hundreds of slaves in the makin'. Should be easy enough. Just head straight for the office, break in and light that fucker up. The rest should take care of itself.

*

Good on ya, mate, you're learnin'. I didn't need to remind ya of the 'road rules', haha. Pull right up to the office. Dawn is fast approachin' and ya want a clean, quick getaway before the world wakes up to another day of slavery. OK, let's do this. Don't forget ya trusty crowbar.

Now, you're gonna need to be quick. You'll have less than a minute to get in there, trash the joint, and light the fucker up before the alarm sounds. This one will be risky, but you've got this. Just smash the glass outta the door, get in and get out.

Fuck! The alarm was instant! Quick, do what ya came to do and let's get the fuck outta here. Plenty of paper in this office to start a nice bonfire, now light it up!

You're efficiency is impressive, haha. Now, let's get outta here before the pigs arrive.

Shit. Sirens. They're onto ya, man, now double-time back to the car. Let's go!

They're here! They've blocked ya in. Only way out is through. There's only one option: fuckin' ram the cunts.

BLAM! BLAM! BLAM!

Keep goin'! Get the fuck away, mate!

Oh shit, you're hit.

Watch out for that pole! Fuck!

Sorry, man. Maybe we were a little hasty with this last venture. I know it hurts. Can you still hear me? Look, you made only a small dent in your journey to freedom, but it was a significant shift in your awakening before 'The Man' came 'n' took it all away. Just keep this in mind as you fade away. You may be dying, but you are leaving this world… a free man.

Japanese Flag
Crystal Jeans

The first time I ever had an orgasm was with my stepfather's electric toothbrush. I remember lying on my bed with the sunlight coming through the window, a fuzzy yellow square warming one thigh, the back of the toothbrush jammed against the nub of electrical flesh I had no name for yet. I remember the usual feelings of frustration and pointlessness giving way to pleasure, then too much pleasure, then a light tingly loveliness spreading through my whole body. Then it was over.

I put the toothbrush back on the shelf above the sink. I didn't wash it.

*

Mum kicked Dad out when I was fourteen. She said he was a useless, worthless man and she'd wasted enough time on him already. She'd recently started evening classes doing aromatherapy and massage therapy, and she'd made friends with a couple of women who wore tie-dye and sandals and lots of silver bangles. They took her along to their Primal Urges dance group, where she stomped and screamed and writhed and panted to African drums. When her divorce papers came through, they celebrated with a ritual on the beach: tits out, kicking sand, dancing around the campfire. She was a new woman. A shamanic divorcee.

Dad was not a new man. Dad was pathetic.

Mum met Andrew six months later at a *Rocky Horror Picture Show* play in the New Theatre. He was dressed as Eddie: blue jeans, motorcycle boots, black leather waistcoat, a red syrupy gash on his forehead. Mum was Columbia: gold-sequined tux, gold-painted top hat, fat arse crammed into tiny hot pants. They fancied each other straightaway.

Mum came home with fake blood smeared over her cheeks and a secret sort of knowledge in her eyes. It bothered me.

*

Andrew came for Sunday dinner. Mum had recently gone vegan. She'd made a tofurkey – tofu and stuffing moulded into a vaguely bird-shaped lump and marinated with soy sauce, garlic and sherry. In theory it was stupid but it didn't taste bad. For Andrew she had bought half a pre-cooked chicken from the Deli at Sainsburys. He gulped down his meal, skin and all. When Mum cut herself an extra slice of tofurkey, Andrew smiled indulgently.

Andrew was thirty-five. He worked in computer programming. He was stocky, not quite fat. Big arms, shoulders like humpback bridges. He wore a faded The Cure t-shirt, black jeans and green Dr Marten shoes. He had black hair combed back Italian-mobster style, a thick-skinned face, big loose lips. He looked like a gargoyle with pretty eyelashes.

After dinner Andrew drank beers in the sitting room while Mum fluttered around like a dumb butterfly. He asked me some questions. How was school? Was I popular? Did I have a boyfriend? What kind of music was I into? I answered obediently: Shit. No. No. Death metal.

"I used to be a bit of a headbanger myself when I was your age," he said. "First gig I ever went to was Megadeth." He looked at me expectantly.

"Who are Megadeth?" I asked.

He frowned. "Only the best metal band of the eighties."

I shrugged and sipped my pop. I knew who Megadeth were. I just wanted Andrew to feel obsolete.

*

At first I wasn't sure why I hated Andrew. Maybe it was the smug smiles he flashed when he thought he was being ironic.

The way he spoke like a politician sometimes. The bits of goo that formed in the corners of his mouth. But it wasn't just these things. Andrew had become Man of the House – the proud lord – and Mum took on her new subservient role with a breathless elation. I didn't like seeing that. The chair at the head of the dinner table became his, along with the armchair closest to the TV. After two months of dating he took over the driving from Mum. Because he knew the road better than her.

He had claimed all the best seats. And Mum loved it. She all but fanned him with lotus leaves and fed him fucking grapes.

The day I realised I truly hated the man was a Wednesday. He came to the house with a bottle of South African wine. He walked into the living room and stopped suddenly, sniffing the air like a hound. "I can smell blood," he said. "Someone's on their monthlies, I'll bet!"

Mum clapped her hands. "Andrew has an *amazing* sense of smell," she told me.

I looked at them with disgust. Andrew was smiling broadly at his clever trick. I put down my homework and went to the bathroom to change my sanitary towel and scrub myself with Mum's face flannel. I felt violated. *What kind of dick is my mother dating?* I thought, squeezing the brown-red water out of the flannel until my hands burned.

*

It took three months for Andrew to move in. He immediately started to redecorate. He painted over her dark reds and deep purples. He favoured oatmeal, milky coffee, biscuit-brown. Fucking ecru. He swapped her Indian rugs for grey shags, took down her Frida Kahlo prints and put up generic sunsets.

"I don't know why I ever bought that thing," Mum said, frowning at the pregnant African lady figurine she'd loved three months ago.

Andrew thought Mum's veganism was 'a bloody hoot.'

"Go on," he said to her one dinnertime, "try this meat and tell me it's not better than that blasted bird food." He held the fork to her mouth. "Go on, have a taste, Meg." She opened her mouth and took the beef between her teeth, sliding it off the fork. "Well?" Mum chewed for a long time, big doll eyes focused on Andrew's face. "Well?" repeated Andrew, smiling.

Mum smiled back. "It does taste pretty good. I can't deny it."

Andrew grabbed Mum's plate with its kidney bean and spinach nut roast and emptied it into the bin. "Of course it does. That's how we know we're supposed to eat it."

I stared at Mum. I knew she'd only gone vegan because of her stupid hippy friends, but it still upset me to see this fickleness so transparently exposed.

Andrew carved Mum a thick slice of bloody cow and placed it in front of her. "Enjoy, sweetheart," he said. He looked at me. "What about you? Fancy eating a real meal for a change?"

"No, I'm happy with my bird food," I said, smile made of glass.

*

Andrew left me alone at first. He was too busy making Mum roar in the bedroom to think about the teenage girl from the previous marriage. But soon he decided he'd better start playing at stepdad. I made this hard for him. If he came into a room I'd vacate it. Mum would take me aside and say, "Why can't you just give him a chance, hun, for me?" or "He's lovely when you get to know him." I'd feign ignorance. "I don't have anything against him, Mum. He's fine."

Sometimes Andrew would loiter by my bedroom door, nodding his head appreciatively to my music. "I like this," he'd say. "Sounds a bit like Napalm Death." I'd look at him like he was a fucking moron and close my door. I wouldn't slam it.

He began to try harder. He suggested we have a movie night

every Sunday, me, him and Mum. Bowl of popcorn, cold cans of pop, curtains closed, lights off. A family. We all came up with film suggestions but Andrew had the final decision. He'd go down to the one remaining Blockbuster in Wales – in Mum's Clio – and return with the DVD and some popcorn like a conquering hero. Because it was a family night, we all sat together on the couch, Andrew in the middle, Mum cuddled up to him. He sat with his legs too wide, his thigh touching mine.

Andrew had this loud braying donkey laugh. He laughed in all the predictable places, at the things stupid people laugh at. The thunderous hee-hawing, the thigh like a warm log of shit – I pushed myself so far to the edge of the couch that I'd end up with red marks on my hips from the armrest.

Afterwards Andrew liked to switch the lights back on and talk about the film. "I didn't believe him in this film – his accent was all wrong." "Did you get the twist? I figured it out within twenty minutes." I never joined in. Just sat there picking dead rubbery skin off my feet, answering his questions with shrugs.

One night, after *District 9*, Mum sighed with exasperation and said, "Well, if you're not going to speak, you could at least thank Andrew for buying the Pringles."

I looked at her. "Is he going to thank us for letting him live in our house?"

Andrew's face went like pickled cabbage. "You shouldn't let her talk to me like that, Meg."

Mum's mouth opened and closed – no words. I ran off to my room, locking the door and turning on my music. A minute later I heard knocking. I shouted, "Leave me the fuck alone!" Silence. Then footsteps, fading away.

I guess that was the point Andrew stopped trying to make me like him.

*

A Saturday night. I came home from my friend's house stoned and hungry. I was planning on a bowl of Cinnamon Grahams with soya milk. I had no love of soya milk and didn't care much about the suffering of animals, but I was determined to keep up with the veganism to piss off Andrew.

The house was quiet when I got in. I went into the kitchen. Mum and Andrew were at the table. Staring at me. There were items laid out in front of them: a bottle of poppers, a half-smoked spliff and two cans of Oranjeboom.

"What the fuck are you doing with my things?" I shouted.

"I found them in your bedroom," said Andrew.

"What were you doing in my bedroom?"

"I was looking for a CD."

"You were looking for a CD in my fucking underwear drawer?"

"I could smell the weed."

"Oh, fuck off. You were snooping."

Andrew glanced at Mum. Mum looked at me desperately. "You're fifteen! And you're doing drugs!"

I scowled. "A spliff and some poppers? Yeah, I'm a real junkie."

Andrew lifted his hand slightly, like a politician at the podium. "That isn't the—"

"You, shut up," I said. I turned back to Mum. "Who are you to tell me off about drugs? Smoking bongs in the living room with those fucking hippies – how can you talk?"

Mum looked down at the table. "I don't do that anymore."

"Exactly," said Andrew. "Things are going to change around here." He sliced his hand through the air. "This is going to stop. Your attitude is going to change." He glanced at Mum. "We're getting married."

"What?"

Mum smiled weakly. "We're getting married." She lifted her chin with something like defiance. "Andrew's going to be your stepdad."

"And you'd better get used to it," said Andrew. "Now go to

your room."

That night I lay in bed for hours imagining Andrew being lubelessly raped.

*

They made me wear a lilac bridesmaid dress. In all the wedding pictures I could be seen staring at the ground hatefully. Andrew smiling and lifting a flute of champagne like a jolly king at a feast. He wore his green Dr Martens with his tux to show how fucking edgy he was. Mum wore a classic white wedding dress, and her auburn hair was curled and covered with white hibiscus. She looked pretty and happy and brainless.

At the reception I sat at a table opposite Andrew's brother, who looked more miserable than me. He had thick black hair and shaving nicks up his neck. He was a better-looking version of his brother but he stunk like onions, sweat and booze. I imagined taking him to the toilets and fucking him, leaving the door unlocked so someone – preferably Andrew and Mum – could walk in and catch me mid-straddle. But this was silly thinking. I was a virgin. I'd never even been touched outside clothes. The brother brooded in silence, hunched over his drink and glancing up resentfully at anyone having fun. After his fifth pint, he got up, staggered off and didn't come back.

Mum tried to make me dance with her to T'Pau and I told her to fuck herself. She looked at me tearfully before running back to her groom. The buffet was full of meat and cheese. There was nothing I could eat. The only crisps were beef and onion. It was a statement. He might as well have had a spit-roasted hog with an apple in its mouth at the centre of the spread. I stared down into my lemonade feeling the fizzy bubbles tickle my chin, my stomach grumbling.

Andrew came over. He was drunk. He put his glass of wine on the table and crouched down to look me in the eye.

"Why can't we be friends? Eh?"

I said nothing. He continued to look at me, head swaying a little. I could hear him breathing loud through his nose.

He sighed, standing up. "Fine. I've tried and tried and still you – Hey, Joey!" His face spread into a greasy smile and he raised his hands in the air. A man came over and they hugged like drunken frat boys, almost toppling over. They started talking and laughing, their backs turned to me.

I looked at Andrew's glass of wine. I glanced at the two men. I quickly picked up the flute and spat into it. I placed it back down. I watched and waited. Without turning his head away from Joey, Andrew reached his hand around, groped for his drink, and picked it up. He took a swig.

To your health, Stepfather.

*

Openly, I'd live by his rules. Secretly, though, I'd fuck them. Small things, I decided. Small victories. I was fifteen. I had no power. It would have to be small things.

My favourite thing was to dismantle Andrew's razors and use the bare blade to cut my thigh. I'd let the scabs form over a couple of weeks, and once they were ready, I'd pick them off and sprinkle them onto his Tuesday bolognese, along with my bogies. My second favourite thing was to do a load of exercises in my room, sneak into his and Mum's bedroom and then mop up the sweat and musk from my arse and fanny with the work shirt draped over the rocking chair. I liked to watch him crinkling his nose and frowning with confusion the next day at breakfast. "I think someone needs a shower," he'd say, not looking at me but meaning me.

I understood I was behaving like a sick person. But this didn't alter my pleasure.

*

One day Andrew came home early from work dripping wet

and in a foul mood. Mum's Clio was being MOTd so he'd had to walk home in the rain (he wouldn't use buses because of some article he'd read about all the germs and fecal particles found in seats). He'd got splashed by fast cars. A tramp had laughed at him. He was tired and coming down with something. He was hungry.

I was lying on the couch. "Oh, poor, poor you," I simpered from over my homework.

Andrew looked at me with acid eyes. He walked over, snatched the book out of my hands and threw it against the wall. "You will not talk to me like shit! I am your stepfather!" He raked his hand through his hair, his cheeks all pouched up with anger. "It's no wonder you're being a cow. You're on your period, aren't you? I can smell it. You're a real—"

"Shut up about my fucking periods, Andrew!"

He leaned over me until his nose was almost touching mine. "I will not shut up!"

He grabbed my ankles and ripped them off the couch. "And get your feet off my fucking furniture!"

I stared at him with cool, dead eyes and slowly walked to my room. I sat on the bed and cried into my hands, the words *fucking hate him, fucking hate him, fucking hate him* repeating in my mind like a siren.

*

I started Googling natural poisons: deadly nightshade, nutmeg, bryony berries, hemlock, aconite root, death cap, cowbane, jimson weed. Too many oysters can cause paralysis. Too much pepper can kill you. Too much water will flush all the sodium out of your body and make you drop dead. Then there's food poisoning – poorly cooked meat, poultry gone bad. *Salmonella, E. coli.* Ingesting faeces can give you worms and sickness.

I researched household poisons. Bleach and ammonia. Oven cleaner. Paraquat. Rat poison. Wood alcohol.

Antifreeze. I read about the deaths – ingesting any corrosive cleaning product will burn through your mouth, oesophagus, stomach. Your stomach acid will be released into the trunk of the body, where it will dissolve your internal organs. Rat poison can cause massive internal bleeding followed by death in large quantities; dizziness, bleeding, nausea, vomiting and diarrhoea in smaller amounts. Drinking antifreeze causes depression followed by heart and breathing difficulty, kidney failure, brain damage and possibly (hopefully) death. I liked that one, the way it starts with depression. I sat crouched over my laptop imagining Andrew getting sad, really sad, and then dying.

I calmed down after a few hours. I thought, *I don't want to kill Andrew. I'm not a murderer. I just want to make him sick for a while.*

*

I ordered some rat poison from China, hoping it would get through customs. It did. A package of white powder, apparently banned from most countries. I didn't want the blue pellets, for obvious reasons. The website had said it would be tasteless, but when it arrived I dabbed the tiniest amount on my finger and tried it. Slightly bitter. Like well-cut speed.

Luckily Andrew had a thing for garlic. Whenever he cooked up a curry or a pasta dish he would crush a whole bulb. I don't know how Mum put up with it. My best friend from school said when her boyfriend ate garlic, it made his cum taste disgusting.

One night he cooked lamb madras from scratch. He got the kitchen stinking of coriander and cumin and garlic and oil. Stirred the bubbling curry while humming along to 'This Charming Man' by The Smiths. He plated up. A large mountain for him, a smaller one for Mum. I was at the kitchen table, pretending to do my history homework. He left the room to call Mum, who was upstairs resting. I got up, took out the bottle of powder from my hoodie pocket and sprinkled some into Andrew's curry. I swirled it around with my finger to make sure it mixed, then ran back to the table before Andrew reappeared. I wiped my hand on my trousers. My heart was beating fast.

Andrew put the plates on the table and sat down next to me. Mum sat opposite us. Andrew poured two glasses of wine and they picked up their forks.

"Aren't you having any with us?" said Mum.

I shook my head.

"You could just pick the meat out."

"The juices will still be there."

"Andrew, you could've made a little vegetable one on the side for her?"

Andrew snorted through his nose. "Why should I go out of my way? Being a vegan is her choice, not mine."

Mum raised her eyebrows and sipped her wine.

I watched Andrew shovel the first forkful of curry into his mouth, my pen frozen in mid-air. He chewed, swallowed. Drank some wine.

"You feeling better?" he asked Mum.

She nodded, her jaw working. "I just needed a nap."

"How's the curry?"

"Lovely," she said.

He frowned slightly. "I think I might've burned the cardamom again. It's slightly bitter."

"It's lovely, Andrew."

He shrugged and sipped some more wine. "It's not bad." Ate another forkful. "Not as nice as that bhuna I made last month though. That was epic." He side-eyed me. "Isn't that what the kids are saying these days? 'That bhuna was totes epic. This madras, though, is blates pedestrian.'"

"Don't try to talk like the yoot, Andrew," said Mum.

"I was being ironic," he said.

"More like moronic," she replied, flashing me a conspiratory smile. Still trying to make us a family. She sipped her wine and watched him eat with smiley love in her massive green eyes.

He ate every mouthful, mopping up the sauce with a naan.

*

It wasn't easy sneaking the powder into his food – sometimes he cooked something bland like mashed potatoes and roast chicken. I wouldn't bother those times. I always waited until he was calling Mum for dinner; I didn't want to poison her. Well, I kind of did. But I wouldn't.

When he made a spicy, garlic-soaked pasta one Saturday night, I used loads, stirring it into his portion with my finger and wiping the edge of the plate with a tea towel to hide the fact the food had been disturbed. He'd drunk red wine while cooking it and was pissed by the time of eating. He didn't notice.

On one occasion he almost caught me. I spun away from his plate and walked with a too-straight back to the fridge, my eyes petrified. It was a nervy business.

After a few days he started getting nosebleeds. He'd be watching TV and suddenly bright red blood would drizzle onto his chin, his chest. Loads of it. Scarlet droplets the size of pennies appeared on the miserable cadet-grey rug. The coffee table became covered with twists of blood-and-snot-tipped tissue. The bleeding took ages to stop. "Must be the eighties catching up with me," he'd joke. Mum told him to see a doctor but he waved her worry away and said he felt fine, nosebleeds were normal. "I used to have them all the time when I was little. It's nothing." After a week he went sickly pale. Large bruises appeared on his arms and legs like thunderclouds.

I watched these developments with a strange mix of guilt, fear and ecstasy. I was going too far.

I *liked* that I was going too far.

*

A Tuesday. Andrew pulled a sicky from work because he felt dizzy. He lay on the couch in a U2 t-shirt and white boxers, one arm hanging limp off the side. Mum pressed her hand to his forehead and told him to see the doctor. "Please, Andrew. I'm worried."

"It's just man flu," he said with a weak smile, a film of blood pinking his teeth.

"I'm going to make an appointment for you," she said, kissing the tip of his nose.

"Good luck with that. Last time I tried calling that surgery, the waiting time was two weeks."

"I'll tell them about the bleeding."

"They won't take it seriously, love. Two weeks, bet you anything."

"I will *make* them take it seriously, Andrew." She looked down at him tenderly. "I'm worried about you."

"I'm a trooper. I'll be fine."

"You are not a trooper. You're a sick man."

"*You're a cunt*," I whispered.

Mum went off to make the call. It was half-term and I was home from school. I was in a pair of tracksuit bottoms and a baggy Fruit of the Loom t-shirt. Daytime TV was on, but I was reading a Poppy Z Brite book about gay vampires. Mum came back and told Andrew he had an appointment with Dr Hunter for half four in the afternoon.

"You're a star," he said.

Her proud pink face, her shining eyes.

"*You're a twat*," I whispered.

*

Mum went to the shop for some 'bits and bobs.' I stayed in the living room with Andrew. We didn't speak. He lay on the couch in his crisp white boxers. His legs were chunky and hairless. When he shifted onto his side, he lifted his leg slightly and I saw his smooth pink bellend in the gap between cloth and thigh. He changed the channel until he found The News. Soon, his breathing slowed down and he was asleep. He had a wad of baby-blue tissue skewered into one of his nostrils.

I watched him closely, elbows on my knees, leaning forward. *Have a good look*, I thought. *This is my stepfather. The man who has taken over the house. The man who has lobotomised my mother with his dick.* I looked at his face. His eyelids were quivering. He was breathing quietly through his mouth. He looked peaceful.

Blood began to drizzle from his free nostril. It ran down his cheek and soaked through the cushion. I felt bad seeing it. I don't know why. Maybe because he was asleep. Powerless.

His leg twitched. I noticed a small red dot like a bindi on the crotch of his shorts. Blood. I watched as it slowly spread into a poppy, then a rose. A lovely red against his white boxers. A Japanese flag.

"Who's on their period now?" I said.

Suck On This, Bitch
Ty Schwamberger

"What do ya think we should do tonight?" Steve asked, taking one last long draw on his Marlboro and then snuffing it out in the butt-filled ashtray sitting on top of the dirty end table.

His friend – hell, his *only* friend – just sat there like a lazy bullfrog, not moving except for the pulsating fat that encircled his neck.

"Hey. Marc!"

"Huh… what?" his friend mumbled, barely turning his head to the left.

"I said, what do you think we should do tonight?"

Marc choked out a phlegmy cough and then replied, "Tonight? Shit, Steve, I don't know… How about one-eight-hundred dial-a-whore?" He laughed; his belly shook like a bowl full of jelly.

"Very funny."

"No, I'm serious," Marc said, trying to sit up straight, his rotund body fighting against him. "Let's dial a hooker or something, man. It'll be a hoot. Hell, it's probably been at least a week since I last called Miss Jena's Escort Service, and I just got my welfare check yesterday, so why not? Fuck, I'll even spring for a broad for you, man."

"Nah, I'm good," Steve replied, standing up from the couch and slinking his boney frame towards the kitchen. Then he shouted from the next room, "Besides, man, don't you think it's wrong to be treating women like that? Like pieces of meat or something. Ya know what I'm saying?"

"Actually, no, I don't, asshole. And hey, grab a knife outta the drawer to cut this pizza. All the damn cheese comes off each time I remove a slice of pie."

"Hey, no need to give me lip service. I didn't do anything to you. Hell, if anything, I probably treat you the best of anyone you know. And yes, I'll get the knife."

Marc mumbled something in return but Steve couldn't understand him from where he was now standing in the kitchen. "Huh?" Steve called out and then pulled open the fridge to grab another brew. He twisted his head to the right and yelled, "Hey, man! You want another brewski or not?"

Nothing.

"The hell with him," Steve muttered under his breath, grabbing one bottle of beer and then slamming the fridge door. "Let the bastard get a fresh one if he needs it. I'm nobody's bitch." He then opened the utensils drawer and pulled out a long, non-serrated knife.

Walking out of the kitchen, Steve twisted off the cap of the beer bottle and entered the small, trash-covered living room.

Marc was holding his cell phone to his ear. "That's right. I'd like your finest two whores for the night." He paused. Then, "Oh… *Oh*! Well shit, bitch… What do you think I'm made out of, money? Fuck that noise." Another pause, a bit longer than the last. Then Marc said in a somewhat depressed voice, "Yeah, OK. I guess *one* Miss Amy will do. But hey, could you make sure she can blow cock like she's sucking the chrome off a trailer hitch?"

After a few more "right", "you got it", "yes, I'll pay cash" type things, Marc ended the call and shouted to Steve, "Get ready, buddy. We've got a bitch coming over and it's a two-for-one deal." He pumped his fat arm into the air and shouted, "Woot! Bitches ain't shit but hos and tricks, yo! Woot woot! It's just too bad that this particular bitch don't know she's gonna get pounded by two guys."

"What?" Steve asked, taking a nervous swig from this beer and then tossing the knife onto the cluttered coffee table. It bounced a few times before coming to a rest next to the open pizza box.

"You heard what I said, fool. The hooker, er, *escort service* wanted to charge me near a grand for two bitches for the night. I said fuck that—"

"No you didn't."

"Well, OK, I didn't actually say 'fuck that', but I was thinking it, ya know? Anyway, the hooker—"

"Escort."

"Ah, yes. Well, the *fine* ladies of the escort service were gonna charge me a ridiculous price for two whores, so we're just gonna have to share one. But hey, no worries. These bitches don't care if they get tag-teamed or not, ya know? Hell, why do you think they call them 'hookers'? 'Cause they're sluts and shit, that's why."

"I don't know, man."

"Hey, what's there to know? She comes over, we give her the six hundred bucks, and then inform her that she'll be getting the purple snake from two instead of one. I'm sure she'll dig it."

"Uh huh. And what if she doesn't, man? I told you before that I still haven't been with a woman, which is one of the many reasons you know why I've never wanted to be with a prostit—"

"Whoa whoa whoa, man. What the hell are you talking about? You letting a whore pop your cherry makes a whole helluva lotta sense. Think about it: when you bust your nut after fifteen seconds, she won't start talking smack about your tiny dick and telling you what a piece of shit you are in the sack. Instead, it'll be 'wham-bam-thank-you-ma'am' and she takes off. Hell, I always knew you were a virgin, and to be honest didn't give a damn, but if you're gonna act like a dry pussy then you might as well just leave now. I mean, if you wanna be a loser all your life, why should I give a rat's ass?"

As if on cue, a dirty, fat black rat scurried across the floor and disappeared under the couch. Steve shook his head in disgust. Sure, he still lived in the basement at his parents' house, but at least he didn't have to put up with vermin possibly nibbling off his toes while he slept. Ugh, he really hated coming over to Marc's place. But the truth of the matter was, he didn't have much choice. He had no other friends and Marc had always been at least somewhat decent to him. Well, better than any other male in his life, including his father, who could be a real bastard sometimes. His mother was a little overbearing at times, but still showed she loved and cared, for the most part. He was at least thankful for that.

With a shrug of his shoulders and a quiet, "Yeah, I guess you're right, man," Steve took another gulp from his beer and returned to the cushion on the couch he had been sitting on. Then he thought two things at once: *I wonder if this prostitute, er, escort will swallow my load, and I hope that rat doesn't dart out from underneath this couch and start gnawing on my Achilles' heel.*

He looked over at Marc, who was sawing away at the cheese on either side of the pizza slice he wanted to devour next.

As Marc lifted the piece out of the box and took a bite, Steve hoped his friend hadn't been able to read the thoughts that had raced through his mind.

*

Amy was only twenty-three but felt twice that age. Fortunately, even though she had been working the streets since she was fifteen, like most of the other escorts she knew, she still looked her age – even if she didn't feel it at times. She still had the face of 'the girl next door' and the body of a Greek goddess. She had long jet-black hair that was straight and ran down to the middle of her back. She had killer eyes and a body any woman, young or old, would die for or be happy to spend tens of thousands of dollars to acquire. Amy was lucky. She had been born that way and hadn't had to kill or pay anyone for her goods.

As she stood in the small bathroom at Miss Jena's Escort Service, she admired her nakedness in the body-length mirror. Her fire engine red corset and black garter belt, thong and stockings were on the floor next to her three-inch-high cherry heels. She knew she was going to look dynamite in them.

She raised the corners of her lips into her trademark sexy smile and then slowly started to trace the perfection that was her form with her small soft hands. She loved the way her body felt, even to herself. Hell, as good as she could make herself feel just by her own touch, she wondered why she ever got into the sex-for-money trade at all. But then she quickly remembered: it was the money, of course, and lots of it.

She ran her hands over her large breasts, down her small, tight stomach and over her smooth tanned hips. Damn, she looked and felt great. She was going to make one single (or married – it really made no difference) fella a lucky son-of-a-bitch tonight. She just knew she'd pop his cork in no time flat. Then it would be off to the next John to get some more well-earned cash.

*

"I still don't know about this, man," Steve said, snuffing out another cigarette in the ashtray and then draining his fourth beer. With him being only one hundred and forty pounds (and that was soaking wet) and a shade over six feet tall, it didn't take much for his skeleton-like body to begin to feel the effects of a few beers, but he didn't care, especially on a night like this one. *Man, I can't believe some escort is gonna pop my cherry*, he thought.

"What don't you know about?"

"All this," Steve replied, standing up from the couch and starting back towards the kitchen to grab another beer from the fridge.

"Geez, man. What did I tell you? It's gonna be great. She'll come over, I'll pay her the money and she'll get it on with us. Hell, we'll tag-team her… even if she doesn't want us to." Marc laughed, his large belly shaking this way and that.

"Whoa, man!" Steve shouted from the kitchen as he grabbed the beer from the fridge and twisted off its top. He threw the cap onto the filthy, crud-caked dishes that filled the countertop and walked back into the living room.

"What?" Marc asked with a smile.

"Don't 'what' me, man. What did you mean when you said, 'even if she doesn't want us to'?"

"What do you think I meant? Hell, I could only afford one whore for the night, and as much as I wanna see you get your cherry popped, I still wanna bust a nut myself. Know what I'm sayin'?"

"Yeah, I guess… but that still really doesn't answer the question, Marc," Steve said, sitting on the couch. He wondered where that disgusting rat had gone, but only for a second. He was more interested right now in what his friend had going on in that high school dropout head of his. He wasn't entirely sure he wanted to know, but figured he better find out just in case Marc had some sort of weird sexual fetish he wanted to do with him, and not only with the woman that was on her way over.

"Oh. Oh, right. Well… say she doesn't wanna get down with both us, right? Well, then we just *persuade* her a little. Now do ya get what I'm saying?"

"Jesus H. Christ on a rubber crutch, Marc. No… No, I don't get what you're saying. Why don't you say it to me in English instead of Hustler language?"

His friend laughed and said, "We *make* her do what we want, man. Money or not. Now do you get it?"

Steve shook his head. Marc smiled and turned back to the scrambled porn they had been watching on the television. Steve wasn't exactly sure he knew what his friend was referring to, but unfortunately he had a good idea. The question was: how far was Marc going to take it? To just verbal abuse (which Steve wouldn't get all that upset with since the chick was still a whore by any other name, regardless of whether she called herself an 'escort' or not), or was more than just hurtful words and semen going to be flying this way and that around the room? Yes, Marc was a real bastard sometimes, but that didn't mean he was a woman beater or anything of the sort. At least Steve hoped that wasn't the case. But at this point, he wasn't going to rule out any crazy future events that might take place in his friend's dirty, small apartment on the upper west side of the shit-smelling city they had lived in since they were young boys, before they had turned into the 'upstanding citizens' they had since become.

*

It was 1986 and they were in high school. Living large (which was sort of an oxymoron, since Marc had *always* been husky), with not a care in the world and all that bullshit. Marc, being two years older but still in the same grade as Steve because he had gotten held back twice – once in middle school and then again their freshman year of high school – had just gotten his driver's license and was allowed to take his parents' old, brown Mercury (which incidentally didn't have Reverse and so you had to be careful where you parked the godforsaken thing or you might get stuck between two parked cars and have to climb out and push the car to get it back to where you could actually go forward in the damn thing) out on Friday night. Marc had pulled up to the curb in front of Steve's parents' house and honked the horn.

"Alright, mom," Steve shouted, opening the first of the two front doors as quickly as he could so he could beat the second blast that was sure to come from Marc's car. "I'll be home… at midnight." He cringed after saying the last word. Not hearing a reply from his mother, who was busy baking cookies in the kitchen for his sister's school bake sale the next day, he smiled, then reached out, grabbed the round handle of the outside door, and gave it a turn.

"Just hold it right there a minute, buster," his mother said, coming from the kitchen and into the long hallway that separated the front and back of the house. She walked within five or six feet of Steve, then stopped. She wiped her batter-covered hands on an already dirty towel. "And where in tarnation do you think you're going, young man? It's already eight o'clock and you haven't even finished your homework."

"But Mom—"

"Don't 'but Mom' me, mister. Where are you and the Erb kid going at this hour anyway?"

"A friend's house."

"'A friend's house', huh? And do this friend's parents happen to be home?"

"Mom! It's Friday night, for Pete's sake! I don't know if they're home or not. Who knows, ya know? They could be out to dinner and a movie like a normal married couple or… I don't know. Heck, Dad's not even here, so why does it matter if Carol's parents are in or not?"

"Ahhh… so now the truth comes out. Carol, huh? You and your friend Marc are going over to a young girl's house when her parents aren't there to keep an eye on you pubescent kids? I don't think so, dear. I don't think it's wise. Besides, if your father ever found out, he would—"

Steve dropped his gaze to the floor, nodded and said, "Yeah. I know, I know, Mom. I know."

"OK. See? So, now do you understand what I'm saying?"

At first, Steve wanted to reply, "Yeah, I get what you're saying, Mom. I know Dad would be pissed that I went to a make-out party, er, to hang out at a girl's house when her parents aren't even around, but I think I might just have a good chance of losing my virginity tonight… and… and if it doesn't happen tonight, it's just never going to happen!" But instead he replied, "Yeah, I get what you're saying, Mom. I really do. OK? What if I promise that if we get there and see Carol's parents aren't home, Marc and I will go over to Bob's Big Boy and grab a burger, fries and a shake? You know you can trust me, Mom. I study hard, even on a Friday like tonight, get good grades, do my chores around the house, and have never lied to either you or Dad." He paused for a few seconds, waiting on his mother's reply. When it didn't come immediately, he said, "So? How does that sound?"

It felt like he was flying as he ran out the second door while shouting, "Thanks a ton, Mom!" He yanked open the passenger door and hopped inside, slamming the car door shut.

Marc gave a half-hearted wave to Steven's mother, who was standing on the front porch of the house with her hands on her hips, giving the car an un-mechanic inspection. When she didn't wave back, Marc thought about flipping the bitch the bird, but then thought better of it. *Shit, I better not. It took his ass long enough to get out of the house and if I get pissy with Mrs. Patterson, she might just yank his ass back inside*, Marc thought and then laughed out loud.

He put the car into drive and slowly pulled away from the curb. He was still smiling half a block away when Steve faced him.

"Geez. What's so funny, asshole?"

Marc shook his head and glanced at Steve. He was a hot dog behind the wheel, even if he had only gotten his license a few days before, but still didn't want to wreck his parents' car on the first night.

"Well?" Steve asked.

"Nothin', man. Nothin'."

"Come on. Why are you laughing your ass off?"

"'Cause, man," Marc said in between chuckles, "it's just funny how your mom was standing on the front porch and shit. She was giving me the evil eye or something. I don't think she likes me very much."

"Big surprise. Do you blame her after what you did to Snuggles?"

Marc stopped laughing, took his eyes off the road as they came to a stop at a red light, and looked over at his best friend. "Hey. I never fucked your cat in the ass, alright? I was sleeping on the floor and the thing must have slinked in through the cracked open door or something."

"True… I'll give you that. But what in the world were you doing humping it like that?"

"Dude! I was *asleep*, alright? How could I stop the little

bastard from climbing onto my legs and curling up on top of my junk? Besides, it's not my fault that your folks named the cat Snuggles, of all things. What did you expect?"

"Maybe. But that still doesn't make much sense. You were moaning and shit. You woke me up, my sister, my parents. I wouldn't have said shit to anyone, even with waking me up in the middle of the damn night, but how was I going to control my folks hearing you ass-raping our cat and them coming into the room and turning the lights on, huh? Shit, man… you had your briefs down around your knees and shit. The cat was howling like… like…"

The light turned green and Marc pressed down on the gas pedal. Out the corner of his mouth, he said, "Like what?"

"Like a cat being fucked in the ass, man! How the hell should I know? I've never heard anything so terrible in my life. Snuggles was making noises like the fucking caged monkeys in the zoo, for chrissake."

Marc started laughing even more at his friend's comment and muttered, "Hey. Like I said, man, I was *asleep*. Penis – er, period!" And then he giggled some more.

"*Riiiiiight*! I'll believe that if I never see the rest of the load you shot up my cat's ass finally ooze out. Until then, you're on your own with my mom. You're a sick bastard. You know that, right?"

"You betcha!"

The boys laughed as they drove the rest of the way to Carol's and all the fun that lay ahead.

They hoped.

*

Later that night, Steve lay in his bed and thought about the night's events: the liquor they had stolen and drank from Carol's dad's booze cabinet in the basement, the lights going out and the black light coming on, the sounds of Marc and Carol kissing and groping, and the pounding of his heart inside his chest as he sat next to Cynthia on the couch. He remembered the way his palms had sweated and how the hair on the back of his neck stood on end the moment Cynthia reached over and placed a palm in the inside of his leg. He could still almost feel the ache in his penis as it filled with blood and grew to massive proportions, wanting, needing a release from the strict confines of his Levi's. And then the sound of his zipper slowly being inched down and the feeling of his penis springing from his underwear like a King Cobra, ready to strike out at its prey. Then came the fondling and sucking.

He could still feel the tightness and wetness of Cynthia's small mouth around his shaft, sliding up and down... up and down. He had so wanted to touch her, rip off her clothes and thrust his manhood into her tight place, but didn't want to take any unnecessary risks of pissing her off and her stopping what she was doing, especially because it felt *so* damn good. He had never kissed a girl before, let alone had a chick give him head, so he sat back and enjoyed the sounds and feelings of what had been happening at that very moment. Of course, when he blew his load inside the girl's mouth without warning, she had gotten a little pissed, to say the least. But by that time he didn't care much. Like most men, he got what he needed, and damn the rest.

Steve smiled and rolled onto his right side to get more comfortable. But his satisfied smile almost instantly gave way to tears when he recalled what Cynthia had said after he blew his load and she was coughing and spitting it up all over his stomach while smacking him at the same time.

"You dirty, rotten, no good son-of-a-bitch, Steve! You shoulda warned me you were about to cum. You almost choked me to death!"

Steve had heard Marc laughing somewhere down in the dark basement.

Since Steve *had* gotten his nut off, he replied, "Why? That's your job, right?"

"Excuse me?" Cynthia had asked in a pissed-off voice.

"You know, 'bitches ain't shit but hos and tricks' and 'lick on deez nuts and suck the dick', right?"

He hadn't been able to see Cynthia's face, but he imagined it had probably been a mixture of hurt, embarrassment and downright pissed off. Of course, the hard slap across his face had pretty much confirmed his suspicions. That, and what she had said while running upstairs to the first floor of the house: "I hope you burn in hell, Steve Patterson! You and your *little* dick!"

The lights had then come on, blinding him. He shook the formation of tears from his eyes and looked over to his left.

Carol had been standing naked with her hands and feet tied behind her to one of the support poles going from the basement floor to the floorboards of the first level of the house.

Marc pinching her nipples with a pair of rusty pliers.

Carol had still been breathing heavy and moaning. Steve wondered why, when the lights were out, he hadn't heard her screaming out in pain, even if he had been occupied by Cynthia's mouth.

But then he'd seen the reason: Carol had been not only tied with rope, but Marc had stuffed a gag into her mouth as well.

As Steve curled into a ball in his warm bed, he remembered Marc saying, "Your turn, my man. Feel free to do with this little whore whatever you wish – anything except fuck her, 'cause they can trace that shit somehow, ya know. Anyway, here ya go." Then Marc had held out the pliers as Steve got off the couch, stuffed his shrunken penis back inside his jeans and zipped up.

Reluctantly (or more just to find out what all he could get away with doing to Marc's girlfriend), he had taken the pliers from Marc's hand and started working on another sensitive area on the girl's body. He made sure to twist the small piece of pink flesh hard as thoughts of what Cynthia had said about his manhood raced through his head.

*

Steve couldn't believe he had suppressed that memory for so long. Now, as he sat next to the same guy he had been friends with since the mid-eighties, he wondered if Marc remembered any of that night's events. He didn't want to ask, though. No way. Because now he knew what his subconscious had been screaming inside his head...

"Hey, Marc."

"Yeah?"

"Would you mind explaining for my feeble mind what you meant when you said we'll still do things to this escort—"

"Prostitute, slut, ho-bag, whore... use one of those words, man."

"Oh, right. Anyway. When you said, 'even if she doesn't want us to'?"

Marc turned his rotund body towards Steve and replied, "Oh, Stevie boy... Always playing by the rules. I think you know *exactly* what I mean. But—"

"But what?"

"But this time, you're finally getting your nut off with a real woman. Well... as long as I bust one first, that is." And then he laughed some more.

*

Amy walked out of the cozy (who was she kidding – the place was the pits) confines of Miss Jena's Escort Service and shut the heavy metal door behind her. The alley, like always, stank of sour urine and stale beer. She stepped over a puddle of what could only be described as a grotesque mixture of semen, piss and beer, and started down the alley. Sure, the escort service wasn't located in the best part of the city, but that wasn't much of a surprise. After all, the shittier the neighborhood, the less likely the service would get busted by the cops. *And if that happens*, Amy thought, *I'll be out on the streets for sure*. Amy only had a tenth grade education. She had dropped out to take care of her dying mother, and hooking was the only thing she knew. Hell, who was she kidding – it was the only thing she was good at, selling what God had given her: the best pussy this side of the river. Hell, maybe the entire city. She was sure of it.

Amy exited the dark shadows of the alley and stepped onto the well-lit sidewalk. She looked from side to side. Nothing; not a bum, drug dealer or another prostitute as far as the eye could see. She turned to the left and started walking. After a block or so of not seeing another living thing, she saw something in the distance. Two even dots starting to come closer and closer – headlights. *At least they're on*, Amy thought, always remembering if you saw a car in this part of the city with its headlights off while it crept down the street, you best take cover in fear of a drive-by – or worse.

Amy knew one escort in particular that got caught up in some nasty shit. From what she could remember of the story, an escort was walking down the street and a car came crawling down the road with its lights off. Whether the girl had been warned or not, Amy didn't know, but when the car pulled alongside her, she hadn't bolted off and hid in the shadows. Instead, she stopped walking, went over to it and bent inside the window, obviously looking for a John that she could blow or fuck for a little extra money on the side. Then, when her head was inside, a man (or so the story went) grabbed her and jerked her into the car. The vehicle then sped away and took the girl to some alleyway where she was tortured, raped, tortured some more, then sliced, diced and gutted, and dumped in some alleyway on the other side of the city – relatively the same area where Amy was supposed to be working tonight.

Amy's bowels tightened as the car continued to inch closer. For a brief moment, she thought about running back the way she had come and into the relatively safe confines of Miss Jena's Escort Service, but there were two problems with that. One, Amy knew if she came back early without taking care of the client that was paying top dollar for her services, Miss Jena would have a fit and possibly even dock the money she brought in from the next John. And two, even if she did make it safely back the few blocks to the alley, raced down the dark area and avoided getting jumped from the shadows or slipping on a puddle of God only knows what, she wouldn't be able to open the door anyway.

Miss Jena had made an almost fail-proof plan for getting her girls to not come back before it was time (i.e., before they blew or fucked the customer – John – and got paid). She did this by giving each customer a one-time unique code that the girls would only learn after they had performed their duties. This was given to each customer over the phone, once they placed their order for the evening but before they hung up. The escort would then have to punch in the code on a special keypad that was bolted on the building's wall beside the metal door. Only then would it unlock. There had been a few instances in the past where the customer had given the escort the incorrect code, either on purpose or by mistake, and as the girl was trying to unlock the door, she had been jumped by a bum or a rival pimp and either beaten, fucked or worse. But, for the most part, the code system worked well for Miss Jena, please and thank you very much.

Finally the car came into view under a nearby streetlamp and Amy was relieved that it was only a taxi and not some crazed gangbanger ready to gun her down, or some loony son-of-a-bitch that wanted to grab her and fuck around with her for a bit before dumping her cold, lifeless body in some stank alley or the river. *No thank you*, Amy thought as she raised one of her skinny arms in the air to hail the approaching cab.

As the yellow-and-black pulled to the curb, Amy heard the pop of the doors unlocking. She walked a few steps, grabbed the handle, opened the creaky-hinged door and got in. She quickly shut it after pulling her legs inside.

The driver, a husky bearded man probably in his late fifties to early sixties, locked the doors and twisted around in his seat to peer through the plexiglass. The man's eyes traced the outlines of her black stockings and garter belt to her tight red corset, smooth neck, and then looked into her big brown eyes. His mouth curved into a twisted smile. "Where to, young lady?"

Amy exhaled the deep breath she had been holding, smiled and said, "1456 Cornwood Avenue. But you can just drop me off at the corner of West 130th and Prospect and I can walk the rest of the way. I don't want my—"

The man's strange smiled disappeared. He looked a mixture of confused and all-knowing, if that made any sense. "Ah, OK. I getcha, miss. No problem." He turned around, put the car into drive, and they started off towards Amy's destination.

Amy hoped she could get her John off in half the time so she could get the hell out of there and onto the next cash-paying client as soon as possible because, as every self-respecting working girl knows, "the more dick you get to squirt in a night, the more money in your pocket come sunlight." At least that was the motto Amy tried to live by, and so far it seemed to be working relatively well.

*

Steve paced while taking the occasional sip from his ever-growing warm beer as Marc shuffled back and forth between the kitchen and the living room. Steve's nerves were shit right now, and watching Marc frantically trying to straighten up the ridiculous mess in the living room wasn't helping matters. He could almost hear his heart pounding inside his chest, could feel the hairs on the back of his neck standing on end and tiny balls of sweat leaking out of the pores on his forehead and streaming down the sides of his face. Some of the salty liquid ran into his eyes; he wiped it away with his free hand. Finally he'd had enough.

"Dude, seriously."

"Huh. What?" Marc said, stopping in mid-stride while

holding an assortment of empty beer bottles, crushed Diet Coke cans and what looked to be some sort of old moldy fruit (Steve couldn't tell what kind).

"Dude, you're scurrying around here like your pet rat—"

"He's not my pet."

"Whatever. You're still running around like a chicken with its head cut off, and to be totally honest, you're making me flip out even more than when I heard what was going down tonight."

"How so?" Marc asked, walking the rest of the way to the kitchen and dumping the junk into the receptacle.

"You're really gonna ask me that? Really? Dude, we have an escort—"

"Hooker, whore—"

"OK… whatever. We have a *hooker*, as you so delicately put it, coming over in less than half-an-hour and we haven't even talked stuff through."

"What do you mean, 'talked stuff through'?" Marc asked, returning from the kitchen and flopping down into his chair with a thud. He inhaled and exhaled a few times, trying to catch his breath. "So?"

Steve took a long swig from his warm beer, draining the bottle, and walked over to the couch and sat down. He looked around the room at what his friend had accomplished in fifteen minutes. Surprisingly, the room looked halfway decent. Not clean by any normal person's standards, but good enough for a bachelor pad. Steve wondered why, if Marc could tidy this much in a short amount of time, he couldn't spend a few minutes doing the same each day. And then he remembered: it was *all* about the sex he was going to be getting soon. Of course it was. Steve had known Marc his entire life and if it wasn't about getting to stick his meat into another tight (or loose, whatever) cooch, then his friend never showed any signs of living a normal life. But, oh boy, when it came to some girl giving it up (or *taking* it from her, which he had told Steve about a time or two), Marc all of a sudden turned into the perfect housekeeper, gentleman and had pockets as deep as Donald Trump. Any other time, Marc was a slob who barely kept himself up, let the trash mound around him and allowed vermin to have the run of the place.

But even with all his flaws, Marc was the best friend Steve could ever wish to have. Sure, there had been times in the past where Marc had made fun of him in public or whatever, but nothing to warrant not being his pal. And sure, there were moments in high school where Marc totally ignored him and let him eat lunch by himself while he was trying to pick up a hot cheerleader (which was never going to happen in a million years anyway). But, all in all, Marc was a good guy – except when it came to sex.

The thoughts of what happened down in Carol's parents' basement started to creep back into Steve's mind. He shook his head to get rid of Cynthia calling his member little, the macabre sexual events that he and Marc had performed on poor Carol that night, and hoped against hope that tonight wouldn't be a repeat. He figured everything would be OK as long as Marc didn't lose his temper when the hooker, er, escort turned down his request at a threesome.

Steven's thoughts were cut short as the intercom on the wall next to the apartment's door started buzzing.

The escort had arrived.

At the sound of sex in the air, Marc shot off his chair and jumped (as well as he could, anyway) up and down, clapping his hands and shouting, "Ding dong, the hooker's here, drain your beer and get ready to get some hair!"

It was a vulgar rhyme that didn't make all that much sense, but Steve figured Marc didn't care about poetry at this point. Marc finished saying his limerick one more time and then headed for the intercom to buzz the escort into the building.

Steve stood up from the couch, put one hand behind his back, interlaced two fingers for hope against hope, and put on his best smile.

Tonight was finally going to be the night he lost his

virginity.

He just hoped he wasn't going to vomit the pizza he had eaten a short time ago in the process.

*

"Hiya, fellas," Amy said as she walked through the door.

Marc shut it behind her. Steve noticed him quietly deadbolt and chain it but didn't say anything. The escort hadn't noticed, as she didn't turn her head. Quickly, Marc came from behind her and walked over to Steve.

"Uhhh…" is all Steve could manage to say. His throat was dry and he wished he had another cold beer to make the itch go away. He could also feel his heart quicken again, and his palms got moist. He slowly wiped them on his pant legs, hoping the girl didn't notice. He continued to smile the entire time, but was scared out of his mind. He didn't know what to expect from her, or worse yet, what Marc was going to do when…

"Well, hello there, young lady," Marc suddenly barked. "You made it in world-class time, and for that, me and my friend thank you."

"My pleasure," the girl replied, looking between the guys. "So, who's getting lucky tonight?"

"Better question is… who's not?" Marc said under his breath.

"Excuse me?"

"Huh? What? Oh… nothing. I said, 'this whore is hot'."

"Oh," the girl replied and scrunched her nose. "I don't get it."

Steve looked from the escort to his friend and then back again. He muttered, "He is," and nodded in Marc's direction.

"Oh. Well, alright then. It's just you and me, big boy. So if you just pay me—"

"Actually…" Marc said, interrupting her.

"Huh?"

"Well," Marc continued, "we were actually hoping for a threesome… of some sort." He smiled.

"Oh," the escort said in a chipper voice. "Well, that's great! My price for two goes up to—"

"One."

"Huh?"

"The price of two is one. It's the simplest math you can do," Marc said, then laughed. His rotund belly shook with each hot breath of air that blasted from his decaying-teeth filled mouth.

"Uhhh…" is all Steve could manage.

"Actually, no it is not. If you boys wanna have a threesome, I'm down for that, but you gotta pay the piper. Besides, double the dick is double the cash. Rules are rules. It's up to you guys, take it or leave it. I'll fuck one of you, but not both unless you have the extra money on hand. Any other arrangements are off the table." The escort crossed her arms over her chest.

"Name is Steve."

"Huh? Fella, I can't hear you. What did you say?"

"He said his name is Steve, bitch. And fuck your rules. Now, get down on your knees and get ready to blow *us*!" Marc barked, unzipping his pants and waddling towards her.

The girl slowly inched her way back towards the door. Steve was pretty sure she still didn't know Marc had thrown the deadbolt and chained it.

Marc looked behind him and said, "Come on, Steve-O. Time for us to get us some sweet, sweet hooker pussy."

He bum-rushed the escort. With his dick half out of his pants, Marc's giant body collided with the girl's tiny frame. Her back slammed against the door, followed by her head. Her eyes rolled back. She hit the floor like a ton of bricks.

Marc picked himself off her and looked at Steve. "Well, man, what ya waiting for? Let's get this slut tied up."

Again, Steve couldn't find the words to describe how he felt or what he was thinking. He couldn't believe what he'd just seen. And then, as he started walking towards Marc and the knocked-out escort, he knew…

Suck On This, Bitch!

It was going to be another one of *those* nights.

*

Amy let out a soft moan. Her eyes scooted from side to side underneath their closed lids. The back of her head hurt and her brain pounded inside her skull. She could feel her heart beating erratically – *thump thump, dump thump*, dump. She was cold and gooseflesh erupted over her body. The sides of her buttocks and breasts felt like someone had jabbed her with a hot poker. Her wrists and ankles were tightly smashed together. She hurt so much that she didn't dare move. As the waves of consciousness continued to wash over her, she started to hear more than just the sound of her adrenaline-induced arrhythmia. All the sounds seemed intermixed, but she could definitely make out a few of them: two men, a woman that sounded like she was having it put to her really good, and another man who was moaning. The man and woman who sounded like they were having a good time seemed to be coming from a television set within the room. The two men seemed close.

Amy finally conjured enough strength to pick her chin off her chest. She felt like she was going to pass out from the spinning inside her head, but had to see where she was now. As her eyelids fluttered open and she saw the meager apartment, she remembered. She had been on a job, and after arguing with the large man that was sitting on the couch next to the skinny one, she had been attacked. His mammoth body had slammed against her, flying her backwards – hitting the back of her head against the door. That's when she must have passed out. *Bingo!*

But now, oh now, as she looked down at her naked and bleeding cut-up body, she knew things were a lot worse than the lump that was probably forming on the back of her head.

"Weeeeell, hello there, missy," Marc said, standing up from the couch and waddling towards the escort.

Even through her blurry vision, Amy could tell that he wasn't wearing any shirt, pants or underwear. The only thing he had on were his white tube socks, which Amy had always thought was a strange thing for a guy to leave on while having sex. Maybe they didn't like their feet getting cold and throwing off their game in the sack? Amy had no idea the reason. In any event, she watched as the fat man continued towards her. She then looked past his rotund, hairy frame and noticed the skinny guy get off the couch. He was completely naked too – no socks on this one. But what he lacked in socks he made up for with something else: he was carrying a blade. From the distance of fifteen or so feet, Amy thought it looked like a steak knife of some sort, but couldn't be sure, not with her eyes still being out of whack.

Both men halted in front of her. Staring. Taking in her nakedness. It must have been quite a sight, as each of them were looking her up and down and licking their lips, their members standing at attention.

The fat man was drooling a little from the corner of his mouth. He glanced over at his counterpart. "So… what do you think we should do with her? You seemed to like cutting her when she was asleep, so if you wanna keep going with that I'm good with it. I can just sit on the couch and watch if ya want."

"Well…"

"Well what, man? This bitch right here is a prime cut of meat." Marc laughed. "I said 'cut'." He giggled some more.

Amy looked at the skinny one and batted her long eyelashes. She wasn't sure if it was going to work, but it was worth a shot. Hell, anything she could do to survive this horrible ordeal was worth a try at this point.

The skinny one smiled for a few moments, but then his smile turned upside down. His eyes went from concerned to bloodshot. He was mad. No… he was pissed. About what, Amy had no idea, and she didn't want to find out. The sad part was, she probably didn't have a choice.

"You don't want a shot at her, man?" the skinny one asked

his partner.

"Nah."

"No?"

"No."

"Why not? You said you wanted to mess around with the escort—"

"Hooker, whore, slut…"

"Right, sorry. I thought you wanted to be the first to stick your dick inside her and everything?"

"Well," Marc said, "I wanted to, sure. But then I saw you in action with the knife and it kinda turned me on, ya know? Never seen a bitch cut like that before. Shit, man, you were slicing away with one hand and had the other buried up inside her and shit."

The skinny guy's frown turned right-side up again, and he said, "Well, I honestly don't know what got into me. I mean, I was watching you pinching her nipples and grabbing her ass. Then when you started to jerk off in front of her… I just lost it. You were shooting your load all over her stomach and I went to work on her with the knife. I guess I was thinking back to when—"

"When what?"

"When that bitch, Cynthia, called my dick 'little', remember?"

"Yeah, man, I remember."

"Killed me, man. I didn't want to even try with another girl till now. But when I saw this hooker tied up to a pole just like Carol had been in her parents' basement, and then throw in watching you rub your chub, I just couldn't take it anymore. I figured you were busy in the front, so that's when I started to slice the sides of her ass and tits a little. It was quite fun, if you wanna know the truth."

Amy turned her gaze towards the fat man. A wide smile stretched across his stubble-covered, pockmarked face. He looked as happy as a father watching his son ride a bike without the training wheels for the first time. He then slapped the skinny one on the back. Hard.

"See man, I knew you could do it. 'Popping your cherry' doesn't always have to mean fucking a bitch for the first time. Sometimes it can mean having them suck you, jerking off in front of them and shooting your wad all over their face or wherever, sticking your fingers inside their pussy or ass, whatever. Then… sometimes it can mean even more fun things than getting butt-assed naked with a whore and messing around with her. Oh yes. Sometimes, you just wanna get naked and rub her shit a little and then fucking kill the bitch and dump her still-warm body in an alley somewhere and…"

The fat man turned his gaze from his friend to Amy. Her eyes opened wide. She wanted to say something, anything, to convince him to not kill her. She wanted to say, "Yes, I'll fuck you both for the price of one, OK? Just please don't hurt me anymore" and "I swear I won't tell a soul about tonight, OK? I promise. I just wanna go home and go to bed. I won't even ask for the price of one, OK? Just fuck the shit out of me any way you guys want and I'll get you both to blow your loads for free, OK? Please? Pleeeeeease!" But nothing would come out of her mouth except for a tiny sob.

She sniffled a few times and looked back to the skinny man. Maybe she could convince him and he in turn would persuade his friend that killing her wasn't worth it, but her pussy was. That she had the best pussy this side of the river and that she could suck a golf ball through a garden hose – just like what all guys want out of a good woman: to fuck, suck and shut the fuck up. She could be their perfect woman, right here, right now, if they would only be so kind as to free her from the hot steam pipe she was tied to. Then she would promise to give *both* of them the best night of their sexual lives. And Amy believed it, too, as she thought it. She knew she was the best. She was The Little Whore That Could. But, she couldn't get her mouth to form any words to say to the skinny one, either.

She wanted to break down and cry but didn't know if that would only anger the men even more, so she closed her eyelids tight to stop the tears from forming and rolling down her cheeks. She felt the anger build inside her. She couldn't stop it – by tear or words, it had to come out.

That was when she blurted, "Whatever chick you were talking about was right. You do have a little dick! And you… oh you, you fat piece of—"

The big man started laughing at the hooker's outburst. The skinny man did not. He had a scowl across his face that she had never seen on a man before, not even from her former pimp she worked for on the streets, before getting hired by Miss Jena's Escort Service. That was when Amy knew she was doomed to end up like the poor girl she had heard about before on this side of town.

She was now *that* girl.

But then her fate seemed to change at the feeling of something biting her left big toe. Before she opened her eyes, she figured it was going to be one of the guys nibbling at it. But, oh no – it was a big, filthy black rat.

Amy's eyes snapped the rest of the way open and she screamed. The rodent continued to chomp away at her bound feet. The tubby man laughed even harder. The skinny man bent over and snatched up the flesh-eating rodent, then smiled as he held the bloody-mouthed creature in one hand and stroked its grimy fur with the other. It made Amy want to throw up instead of scream.

When the thin man stopped petting it and inched it towards her face, she wished she would have.

*

Amy always knew the risks of doing the kind of work she did, but before now had been one of the lucky ones (besides a few beatings by her aforementioned street pimp) who had survived all the crazies that ordered up escorts at all hours of the night, in all parts of the city. She had even visited this side of town a time or two, although this was her first time visiting a John in this particular neighborhood – where a couple of dead girls had been found over the past few years. But crazies could be anywhere, and Amy knew it: the grocery store, a church, in a house with a cheating husband while the wife was away on business and he could do things with her that his wife never allowed, a dark street where a homeless person could jump her, a passing car from which a homeboy could mow her down, and, apparently, in an apartment building with two weirdos with a rodent fetish.

"Wh-what you gonna with that thing, mister?" Amy managed to say after she finally stopped screaming. She couldn't do anything about the tears now. They were streaming down her cheeks and falling off her chin and hitting her bleeding breasts. The droplets splashed onto the floor without a sound.

"Well," the skinny man said, really speaking to her for the first time, "didn't you make a remark about my 'little' dick?"

"Well yeah, but—"

"But *nothing*!" the skinny man screamed into her face.

Amy cried even harder with the man's sudden outburst. She watched through tear-filled eyes as the naked fat man waddled over to the couch and sat down. He grabbed his turtlehead-penis with one hand and started working on it.

"Please…"

"Don't 'please' me, you slut! I bet this here rat is cleaner than your diseased pussy. Glad I didn't stick my dick in there. Who knows what sort of infection I'd get. I'd rather stay a virgin forever than—"

"What did you just say?" the girl interrupted.

"I said, I'd rather stay a virgin…"

"Yeah, that's what I thought you said. Listen," Amy said, trying to choke back the tears to reason with the man, "I'm sorry for saying something about your manhood. Really, I am. I was just scared, ya know? But now… ooohhh, now, since I've got a good look at you and that fine piece of danglin' meat in between your legs, I think we can make it work. All you have to do is untie me and—"

"Shut up, you dirty lying whore!"

Amy snapped her mouth shut. Her half-baked plan had failed (not that she was all that much surprised) and the tears that had stopped for a minute or two started to flow once again. "Pleeease…"

"'Please' nothing! All you whores are the same. You say you like or love a guy and then treat them like a piece of shit. You lie, cheat, steal from our wallets when we're not looking, and just because you might have some fine lookin' titties or a nice big ass we can hold onto while we fuck you from behind, you think you can get away with anything. You sluts even think you can insult us and we won't do a damn thing about it. All you women are whores of one kind or another, either with your mouths or what's in between your legs. But, you know what…"

The skinny man paused. It was enough time for Amy to glance to her right. The fat man was still stroking away. By the looks of it, he was getting close to climaxing.

"Well, I'll tell you 'what', you skank," the skinny man continued. "I for one ain't gonna take it anymore. So… for all the guys *you women* put down and love to shit all over…"

Amy opened her mouth to say something, anything to try to calm the crazed person in front of her.

"…you can…"

The words felt like they were trapped in her throat and she couldn't get them out fast enough.

"…suck on this, *bitch*!"

The skinny man stuffed the dirty rat into her mouth. She could feel the thing's front claws scratching, slicing the tender flesh of her tongue.

Gagging and helpless, Amy looked at the fat man on the couch. White ribbons shot out the tip of his engorged penis. Something hot and wet splashed against her belly. She looked down past the rear end of the rat that was still trying to scurry into her mouth and saw that the skinny man had shot his load all over her stomach.

The fat man shouted from the couch, "See what I mean, man. Getting your cherry popped can mean all sorts of things!"

Then both men started chanting in unison, "Suck on this, bitch! Suck on this, bitch! Suck on this, bitch!"

Through the men's throes of orgasm, the rat burrowed the rest of its fat body into Amy's mouth and tunneled towards her stomach.

Lex Non Scripta
Adam Millard

Lex Non Scripta [leks-non skrip-tuh] noun, *Law*
Latin: Law Not Written – Custom or Common Law

**Southampton, Dec 7.—Survivors of the
RMS Amphitrite, which sank shortly after
its departure last month, have declared that
there was ample time to organise a system
of rescue before the vessel sank, but that the
officers and crew abandoned the ship, where-
upon panic ensued...**

William Shaw read the article in its entirety three more times
before realising the severity of the matter. As he did so, the
hustle and bustle of the pub around him continued, its patrons
unaware they were sharing a room with a murderer. A soon to
be hanged man.

And, worst of all, a *coward*.

The newspaper – as it was wont to do for purposes of
sensationalism – had omitted several key facts of what
transpired upon that dreadful night five weeks prior. There was
no mention of the two children Shaw had managed to drag
from the lower deck, their clothes sodden, their eyes red with
tears. He had piled them into a separate lifeboat before
promising them that the current would lead them to safety. He
recalled the terror upon their tiny faces as they drifted off into
the chill darkness; the loss of their parents would haunt them
forever. Of course, there had been no news of those two
children or whether they had survived. Perhaps they, too, had
perished? Shaw doubted he would ever find out.

Likewise, in the article there was nary a reference to the

casino door, through which Shaw and his crew could not gain entrance despite their best efforts. A hundred souls had been gambling in that room; a hundred souls had never left that room.

Shaw shuddered; the room felt all at once cold, and yet there was a roaring log fire to his right, its flames licking and crackling as fiercely as they had been upon his arrival at the pub an hour before.

Across the room, laughter broke out. A cacophonous gaiety that both startled Shaw and enraged him, for he didn't deserve to be surrounded by such happiness, not after what he and his crew had done, the loss of lives they were indubitably responsible for. He should be made to suffer, the way those – according to *The Courier* – two hundred and seventy-eight men, women, and children were made to suffer.

With his life.

"Anyone sitting there, fella?"

The voice was gruff, and for a second Shaw thought the Devil had caught up with him already and was here to prepare and transport him to his new lodgings, in Hell. But when Shaw looked up he was relieved to discover the man standing before him was one with whom he was already acquainted.

John King was one of the pub's longest-serving punters, a wise and erudite gentleman whose love for billiards was only mired by infirmity. King and Shaw had spoken upon several occasions, had shared drinks on several more. He had a friendly face, and a friendly face was precisely what William Shaw needed tonight.

The hangman's noose, with which he had an appointment in the very near future, would not be anywhere near as amiable as the man before him now.

"John!" he said, somewhat exaggeratedly. He motioned to the empty chair across the way. "Please, take a seat! Might I buy you a drink?"

Resting his cane against the table and placing a tankard – his own silver tankard, engraved with his initials in beautiful scrolling cursive – down upon it, King declined Shaw's offer with a dismissive wave. "I shall be up all night on the bedpan," said he. "No, this is my first and last of the evening, and let's hope it's not the straw that breaks the donkey's back, as they say." He laughed as he sat, removing a woollen scarf from his neck and a brown fedora from his head.

Shaw was all at once pleased of the company.

It did not last long, unfortunately, for no sooner had King sat himself down than he was tapping at the newspaper with a skeletal and arthritic finger; his nails, Shaw noticed, were filthy with grime. "Terrible thing, that," he said with a shake of the head. "A tragedy beyond measure. One might only hope that the spineless crew are brought to justice for their cravenness." As he spoke, spittle flecked the dark, scratched surface of the table.

For just a moment, Shaw panicked. Next King would recall their conversation from the summer in which Shaw had, in a drunken stupor, announced his occupation to the man in order to gain his approval. He wanted King to like him, to respect him, and what better way to gain that respect than to disclose his profession. Captain of a liner was an admirable vocation. Suitably impressed, King had proceeded to buy rounds for the remainder of the evening, until they were both reasonably soused and ready for their respective beds.

Drunk? They were *drunk* that night. Perhaps King had forgotten. Maybe the old man's insensate state at the time had wiped his memory clean, and thusly Shaw was still safe sitting across from the old man while his rage grew.

The more King talked, the more Shaw realised that was the case, and he relaxed a little, certain his secret was safe.

"A captain goes down with his ship," King exclaimed matter-of-factly before taking a long hard slug of his ale and slamming the tankard down upon the table. "That's how it's supposed to be. Save the passengers or die trying. No, those men" – he tapped the newspaper article once again – "were lily-livered and unfit to steer a carriage, let alone a liner filled with souls."

Shaw laughed nervously. "I'm sure they were just frightened," he said. "Who *knows* what goes through a man's head when he is presented with his own mortality."

It was King's turn to laugh, and as he did his face contorted into something monstrous. His bare gums were black and glistened from the light of the fire in the fireplace. "A bullet would be my guess, once the Old Bailey gets hold of them." He laughed again, one eye open and firmly trained upon Shaw while the other was tightly clenched. When he was done – and it took him quite a while to compose himself – he took a sip of beer before continuing. "No, rules are rules," he said. "The crew of that ship – I can understand why they fled so rapidly, but the captain! The captain goes down with the ship!"

Was that an accusatory tone in King's voice, or just Shaw's paranoia? Did the old man recall more from that drunken night in the summer than he was letting on?

If he did, he was being rather cruel, Shaw thought.

"I must be going," Shaw said as he gathered his newspaper up, finished his drink, and went to stand.

"So *soon*?" King said. And then, "Oh, yes, that's right! You like to leave at the earliest possible opportunity, don't you!" His laughter now was drenched with derision, and it was that moment Shaw realised his former drinking partner knew.

He knew, because perhaps he hadn't been as drunk as Shaw had perceived him to be that night. King knew that Shaw was accountable for the deaths of almost three hundred people, and all because Shaw had wanted to impress by imparting his honourable career upon the man.

"Please," Shaw said, barely more than a whisper and leaning into the elderly gent. "Please, don't tell anyone. Only you know. Oh, please tell me you have not told anyone else that—"

"I've told no man," said King, the mirth gone from his face. "And yet I'm not the only man that knows."

Shaw's heart caught in his throat; across the room a glass

smashed and a scornful cheer went up about the place. "Who?" he said, so close to King now that he could smell the ale upon his breath and the stale tobacco in his breast pocket. "Tell me! Please!"

"*You*," said King. A crooked finger came up, punched against Shaw's shoulder with a force belying his age and maladies. "*You* know, and you must *live* with that. *Can* you live with that?"

Straightening up – his back cracked as he did so, and he hissed through his teeth – Shaw regarded the man with an amalgam of contempt and gratitude; contempt for mocking him so unceremoniously, and gratitude for letting the news go no further, at least amongst the regulars of *The Wild Boar*.

"I *have* to," he finally said. "For as long as the good Lord allows it."

And with that he turned and fled the place, never to return.

*

"The captain goes down with his ship!" Shaw said contemptuously as he poured a stiff brandy and tamped his pipe. Who was King to tell him what was expected of him? It was an unwritten law, more for guidance and the peace of mind of the passengers than anything. "Rules! Rules! It's not even a law, and should they come for me I shall be ready!" He lit the pipe and exhaled a thick, sweet plume into the study.

It was not as if he was *responsible* for the fire in the 'First Class' lounge that had initially brought the liner to a grinding halt and then proceeded to sink her over the course of several hours. *If that had been the case, sure, hang me. Tie me to a post and shoot me until nothing remains of my head. I refuse to put up a struggle and will be on my merry way to Hell before you can say Amphritrite.*

But Shaw had been as innocent as every one of those passengers. He had the right to survive, too. A lot of people had made it away on the lifeboats in one piece. *Can't we all just be thankful for that, at least?*

After building and lighting a fire, and topping up his brandy, Shaw felt promptly better. The unfortunate conversation he and King had shared at the pub was already fading in his memory, like a painting left in the sun for too long, although he knew he would never return to that place for fear of being confronted by the ire of a hundred drunken men.

No, he would surely have to find a new watering hole, one where his secret would remain just that.

"I shall take it to the grave with me."

Just then, from the hallway, there came an odd noise, and Shaw verily started, for he was alone in the house. Was always alone in the house.

Perhaps, he thought, *I have left the front door ajar*. The wind had buffeted him along the street as he journeyed home, and it was certainly strong enough to cause such a noise, if one were to accidentally leave one's door open.

But when he arrived in the hallway only to discover that the door was in fact shut – and not only that but locked and bolted in three places – he could only ascribe the noise to his burgeoning paranoia.

The fear that soon, perhaps the next day or the one after that, someone would come for him. Between now and then there would be a lot of mysterious sounds about the place. (That's why they call it paranoia, boys and girls.)

Satisfied he was alone in the house, Shaw returned to the study for a top-up. The fire, which had been burning fine just a moment ago, had inexplicably gone out.

"I'll be damned." Shaw left his empty glass upon the counter and walked across to the still-smouldering fireplace, intent on relighting it on such a cold and inclement night. Yet as he crouched, he saw that the fire had not gone out of its own volition. The fireplace was soaked, as if someone had snuck past him in the hallway and hurled a bucket of water over the whole thing. Water dripped down from the mantelpiece, and each of Shaw's various trophies and knick-knacks had also been saturated during the incident.

He stood and turned, suddenly aware that this was a work of desecration, and therefore he was not as alone in the house as he'd previously thought.

"Hello?" His voice cracked; he did not like the sound of it at all. It sounded weak, vulnerable. But was that not what he was?

He thought about calling out a second time, but instead decided to take up the loop poker from the stand upon which it had been hanging.

Someone had the gall to come into his house in the middle of the night and play games with him. Just thinking about it turned his blood to lava; whoever it was had made a colossal mistake, for William Shaw was now armed and half-drunk. It was this combination that lessened the intruder's chances of making it out uninjured.

Into the hallway Shaw went, the poker held just in front of him, where he would be able to work up a decent swing should the housebreaker suddenly reveal himself. Though his heart was racing so very quickly, he didn't feel the least bit threatened. It was adrenaline – the *good* stuff – which kept him moving along the hallway. That and the thought of catching the intruder in the act.

Something creaked upstairs; Shaw recognised the sound as belonging to his bedroom, for he stepped upon the very same floorboard at least three times a night.

Something exploded within him. Not only had his house been entered unlawfully, but the criminal was now upstairs, in the most sanctified room. The room in which he slept. The room in which he undressed and, though not for many years now, engaged in amatory acts with members of the opposite sex.

Creak.

Shaw could take it no longer. The thought of some assailant up there, amongst his things, was too much to bear. Hastening his step, he made his way toward the foot of the staircase, and that was when he noticed the wet footprints, for that was where the carpet of the hallway came to an end and gave way to bare wooden steps.

So many wet footprints were there that water dripped over the lip at the front of each step. And now that he could see the full length of the hallway, he became aware of the single set of wet footprints leading into and out of his study, right there upon the carpet.

Common sense urged him to telephone for the police, but the last thing he wanted was an army of bluebottles scouring the place for evidence, not whilst he was trying to keep a low profile.

He began to climb the staircase; water splashed slightly beneath his shoes, but he was determined to get the bottom of this, and he had come this far.

As he reached the landing he raised the poker once more, for a faint glow framed his doorframe, as if someone within had lit one of his bedside lamps. The door was slightly open, too, and thin puddles of water trailed all the way across the landing toward it.

Now, and for the first time since discovering the extinguished fire, William Shaw was apprehensive.

What if the person beyond the door had a gun? What if there were two intruders, or three, four? He was certain he would give them a run for their money for a second or two, but after that he would surely be subjugated. Was it not better to simply allow them to take what they had come for and make good their escape? Perhaps hide away in the cupboard under the stairs until it was all over?

Coward! Just like you were a coward when you saved yourself over your passengers, over much of your crew!

Shaw walked steadily toward his bedroom door. The sodden carpet beneath his feet squelched, and it reminded him of the sound the two children had made as he'd plucked them from the arms of their dead parents on the lower deck of the *RMS Amphritrite*, meaty and yet wet all at once.

He struck the thought from his mind and, upon arriving at the door, reached for the knob. As his hand wrapped around it, a cold chill coursed through him, for the doorknob was just as wet as the carpet, staircase, and half-burned coals in the fireplace downstairs. In fact, now that he was just a few inches away, he saw that the entire door was leaking water. It dripped down from the frame above, down the sides and across the hinges. It even poured through the keyhole and pattered gently upon the tops of his shoes.

This can't be! This simply cannot be!

And yet he knew that it was, for the building went no higher, which ruled out any possibility of the water coming from somewhere else.

And as he turned the doorknob and eased the door inward, a seven-foot-high wall of water greeted him. Defying all rules of physics, it just stood there, as if waiting for Shaw to make his move first. Within the murky water – was that sea-salt he could taste upon his lips? – bodies danced around, their broken bones and severed limbs entwined in some sort of Danse Macabre.

That was when he saw them, the parents whose children he had snatched away only to desert once again at the nearest opportunity. Their faces were contorted with grief, not for the loss of their own lives, but for the loss of the two beings – one twelve, the girl, and the boy perhaps eight – wrapped around their waists in one final wet embrace.

Shaw staggered back, the poker falling from his grasp, for all his strength had gone at the sight of such an impossible marine construct.

He did not reach the top of the stairs before the water gave chase, and within it the passengers whose lives had been forsaken in exchange for his own, five weeks prior aboard the *Amphritrite*.

When John King had asked him, not three hours ago, if he could live with what he had done – the cowardly abandonment of those passengers so that he might continue to exist, if only until death caught up with him – he should have told the man no.

He could not live with it.

The water swallowed him whole, but the real devouring didn't begin until the rotting and bloated passengers of the *Amphritrite* were good and ready.

about the authors

Richard Chizmar is the founder/publisher of *Cemetery Dance* magazine and the Cemetery Dance Publications book imprint. He has edited more than 30 anthologies and his fiction has appeared in dozens of publications, including *Ellery Queen's Mystery Magazine* and *The Year's 25 Finest Crime and Mystery Stories*. He has won two World Fantasy awards, four International Horror Guild awards, and the HWA's Board of Trustee's award. Chizmar (in collaboration with Johnathon Schaech) has also written screenplays and teleplays for United Artists, Sony Screen Gems, Lions Gate, Showtime, NBC, and many other companies. He is the creator/writer of Stephen King Revisited, and his third short story collection, A Long December, is due in 2016 from Subterranean Press. Chizmar's work has been translated into many languages throughout the world, and he has appeared at numerous conferences as a writing instructor, guest speaker, panelist, and guest of honor.
facebook.com/richardchizmar
twitter.com/richardchizmar
Instagram.com/richard_chizmar

Fox Emm is a freelance writer living in the Southern US with two tiny dogs. She loves all things spooky and can be found at **BloggingOnward.com**, **wattpad.com/user/foxemm** and on most social media. Loves writing horrible death scenes, networking, and devouring new fiction.

Toneye Eyenot writes tales of horror and dark fantasy which have appeared in numerous anthologies over the past two years. He is the author of a clown/werewolf horror novella titled *Blood Moon Big Top*, released with JEA Press, plus the ongoing *Sacred Blade of Profanity* series with two books, *The Scarlett Curse* and *Joshua's Folly*, also published through J. Ellington Ashton Press and a third currently in the works. He is the editor of the *Full Moon Slaughter* werewolf anthology, and the upcoming *Full Moon Slaughter 2: Altered Beasts* anthology, also with JEA. Toneye lurks in the Blue Mountains in NSW Australia, with the myriad voices who tear the horrors from his mind and splatter them onto the page.

facebook.com/Toneye-Eyenot-Dark-Author-Musician-1128293857187537

toneyeeyenot.weebly.com

twitter.com/toneyeeyenot

Suzanne Fox is a writer of both horror and erotic fiction which she manages to fit in around her day job as a nurse. She grew up in Staffordshire, England before moving, eleven years ago, to the beautiful county of Cornwall where she lives with her partner and three pussies: Cats, you dirty-minded folks! She loves the challenge of combining erotica and horror in her writing. Her work has been published in both print and online magazines with her short story "Hitting the Jackpot," coming third in a writing competition run by Writer's Forum. She has also had stories appear in several anthologies. Besides writing, she loves to dance, and drink wine with friends. She had great fun writing her story, 'The Punishment Room,' and she hopes that you have as much fun reading it.

facebook.com/suzannefoxerotica

Rose Garnett's first novel in the *Dead Central* series, *Carnalis*, is to be published by Permuted Press on March 27th 2018. For those of an infernal disposition, her short stories can be found in four other anthologies; *Man Behind the Mask*, *Collected Christmas Horror Shorts*, *What Goes Around* and *Psychic Detectives Vol IV*, with a fifth, in *The Big Book of Bootleg Horror Volume 2*, awaiting publication. She is currently working on the second book in the *Dead Central* series, entitled *The Charnel House*. Story fragments lifting the oubliette on Rose's world can be found on her blog at **rosegarnett.com**

Crystal Jeans is a Cardiff-based writer and the author of two novels: *The Vegetarian Tigers of Paradise* and *Light Switches Are My Kryptonite*. She's not a known horror writer but her stories are usually gross.

Adam Millard is the author of twenty-six novels, twelve novellas, and more than two hundred short stories, which can be found in various collections, magazines, and anthologies. Probably best known for his post-apocalyptic and comedy-horror fiction, Adam also writes fantasy/horror for children, as well as bizarro fiction for several publishers. His work has recently been translated for the German market.

Skip Novak is a just turned middle aged, non-award winning, over grown man-child who is paid to play with toy trains. In his off time, he enjoys spending time with his wife and daughter, riding his Harley, affectionately named Bernadette and writing. He's been published in some pretty cool anthologies that were put together by deranged derelicts. If you want to contact him, against any better judgement, you can find him on Facebook, twitter or even his blog, **aloysiousthoughts.blogspot.com.**

Ty Schwamberger is an award-winning author & editor in the horror genre. He is the author of a novel, multiple novellas, collections and editor on several anthologies. In addition, he's had many short stories published online and in print. Three stories, "Cake Batter" (released in 2010), "House Call" (released in June 2013) and *DININ'* (optioned in July 2013), have been optioned for film adaptation. He is an Active Member of the International Thriller Writers. **tyschwamberger.com**

Antonio Simon, Jr. is an award-winning author of six books and over thirty short stories published to date. His debut novel, *The Gullwing Odyssey*, is a fantasy-comedy that became an

Amazon Kindle Top 5 Bestseller in 2014. He has won the prestigious International Book Award; the Royal Palm Literary Award; the Pacific Book Award; Indie Book of the Day; and the Reader's Favorite Five-Star seal. Mr. Simon holds a law degree from Saint Thomas University School of Law and two undergraduate degrees (Political Science and History) from the University of Miami. He lives in Miami, Florida.

gullwingodyssey.com

Guy N. Smith had his first short story published at the age of 12 and subsequently went on write over 100 books. Genres include: horror, mystery fiction, westerns, children's fiction and non-fiction titles. He has also penned many short stories for anthologies and the legendary London Mystery Selection. He began writing for the sporting press in 1963 and is still a contributor to 'The Shooting Times' and others. Guy and his family moved to the Shropshire/Welsh border hills in 1977 where he acquired 7.5 acres of steep pastureland adjoining his house. Passionate about the countryside and conservation he created an organic small holding along with a compact old-fashioned rough shoot which took many years to complete. In between writing he has had a varied career, he worked in banking, was a private detective and had his own shotgun cartridge loading business.

about the editors

David Owain Hughes is a horror freak! He grew up on ninja, pirate and horror movies from the age of five, which helped rapidly install in him a vivid imagination. When he grows up, he wishes to be a serial killer with a part-time job in women's lingerie… He's had several short stories published in various online magazines and anthologies, along with articles, reviews and interviews. He's written for *This Is Horror*, *Blood Magazine* and *Horror Geeks Magazine*. He's the author of the popular novels *Walled In* (2014) & *Wind-Up Toy* (2016), along with his short story collections *White Walls and Straitjackets* (2015) and *Choice Cuts* (2015).
david-owain-hughes.wix.com/horrorwriter

Jonathan Edward Ondrashek is an Operations supervisor by day and moonlights as a horror/dark fantasy writer. He's the author of The Human-Undead War Trilogy (*Dark Intentions*, *Patriarch*, and *A Kingdom's Fall*). His short stories have appeared in numerous horror anthologies, including the highly acclaimed *VS: US vs UK Horror*. He also co-edited *What Goes Around* and *Man Behind the Mask*, two anthologies featuring work from stellar established and new voices in the horror genre. If he isn't working at his day job, reading, or writing, he's probably drinking beer and making his wife regret marrying a lunatic. Feel free to stalk him on social media. He loves that shit.
jondrashek.com
facebook.com/jondrashekauthor
twitter.com/jondrashek
instagram.com/jondrashek

Printed in Great Britain
by Amazon

27338661R00118